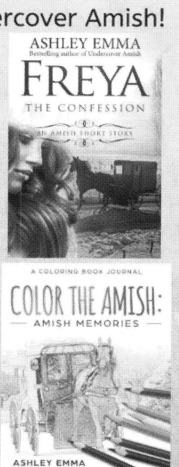

Other books by Ashley Emma on Amazon

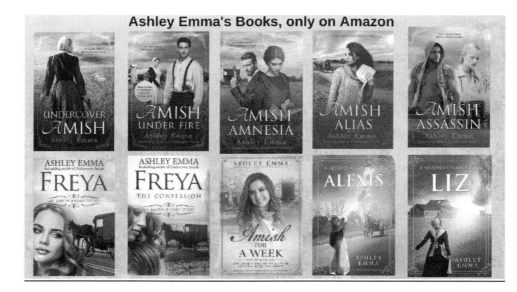

Coming soon in the Amish Fairytale Series:

SPECIAL THANKS TO:

Julie

Abigail

Kit

Gail

Robin

Aurelie

There were so many readers from my email list who gave me helpful feedback on this book, so I couldn't list you all here. Thank you so much!

Check out my author Facebook page to see rare photos from when I lived with the Amish in Unity, Maine. Just Search for 'Ashley Emma, author and publisher' on Facebook.

Join my free Facebook group 'The Amish Book Club' where I share free Amish books weekly!

The characters and events in this book are the creation of the author, and any resemblance to actual persons or events are purely coincidental.

AMISH SNOW WHITE

Copyright © 2020 by Ashley Emma

Amish Snow White

Ashley Emma

TABLE OF CONTENTS

CHAPTER ONE

This can't be happening. I should have done more to stop this.

Adriana Daniels felt as though her world was slipping out from under her, tilting and careening, as she knocked on the door to her dead sister's mansion.

Dead. Her sister, Jordan, was dead. Ever since she'd received the call, she felt as though she was walking through a fog.

Mrs. Clement, the friendly housekeeper who was more like family, answered the door. "Oh, my dear," the elderly woman said, pulling Adriana into a tight hug. "I am so sorry."

"I got here as quickly as I could. He did this, didn't he?" was all Adriana could whisper. "He killed her. I know he did."

Mrs. Clement held Adriana at arm's length. "Right now, the police seem to be agreeing with Henry that she fell down the stairs by accident, but I heard Henry and Jordan arguing right before she died. I think he pushed her."

Anger toward her brother-in-law flamed within Adriana. "I knew he was abusing her all this time. I should have tried harder to convince her to leave with Megan."

"You did everything you could. She made it clear she wouldn't leave. I think she was afraid he'd kill her if she did."

Adriana nodded in agreement. "Is she... Is she still in there?" she asked in a shaky voice, part of her not wanting to know the answer.

"Yes, but they are about to take her away."

Mrs. Clement stepped aside, and Adriana willed herself to move forward. Adriana barely noticed the police milling around the house as she made her way inside. On a gurney, beneath a white sheet, was her sister's body. Before she realized what was happening, Adriana was running.

"I'm sorry, Jordan. I'm so sorry," Adriana sobbed, reaching out to touch her sister's body. "I tried. I should have done more."

"I'm sorry, ma'am. I have to ask you to step back," an officer said, holding his hand up to stop her from touching Jordan's body. "This is an official death investigation. Can I get your name, relationship to the deceased, and contact information for the detectives?"

She gave him the information as guilt moved into her heart and made a home there, growing with each passing second. Would it ever leave?

Adriana caught movement in the corner of her eye. Megan, her thirteen-year-old niece, stood at the top of the stairs, her light blonde hair falling around her shoulders in waves.

Adriana had been so focused on her own pain that she'd almost forgotten how much more Megan must be hurting. The poor girl had just lost her mother, and her stepfather clearly didn't care about her.

"Angel!" Megan called, arms open, and Adriana's heart warmed a bit at the nickname Megan had called Adriana since she was a child, when she'd been unable to say "Adriana."

Adriana hurried up the stairs, embracing her niece into a hug. "I'm so sorry, Megan."

"This isn't your fault," the girl said in a small voice.

It felt like it was.

"I can't believe she's gone. Now I'm all alone here. I wish I could come live with you. I hate it here, living with my stepfather. With Mom gone, I don't want to be here with him anymore."

"I know, sweetie. But I can't just take you away. Henry would call the police and tell them I kidnapped you. Has he hurt you?"

"No. He never hurt me, only Mom. I don't think he will. He just ignores me or yells at me, and I feel so alone. At least I have Mrs. Clement." Megan sniffed and pulled away, and they went into Megan's room and shut the door.

For several minutes, Megan and Adriana held each other, sobbing. Finally, Megan wiped her tears and pulled away.

"Did you see what happened?" Adriana asked.

"No. I was in here doing homework. I heard them arguing, then I put on headphones to listen to music. But I know he pushed her down the stairs." Megan fingered the heart-shaped pendant that hung around her neck, a nervous habit. "He's almost done it before."

Adriana nodded. "I think he did, too. So does Mrs. Clement."

"How can we prove it?"

"I don't know," Adriana said. "I'll figure out a way."

Someone knocked on the door.

"Open this door," a male voice said. Henry sounded calm, but Adriana knew that if there were not people downstairs, he would use his normal booming voice.

Megan's eyes widened with terror, as if Henry had tried to break the door down. "We better do it."

Though Adriana wanted to hide under the bed like a child, she went to the door and opened it.

Henry, her late sister's husband and Megan's stepfather, stood in the doorway, disdain in his coal-gray eyes. "Of course, you're in here. I don't want you filling Megan's head with nonsense. You need to leave right now."

"You're going to make me leave my sister's house after what just happened? I came to pay my respects."

"And conspire with this one," Henry said, gesturing toward Megan dismissively. "Her mother just died from a horrible accident. Let her grieve in peace."

"Accident?" Adriana whispered. Though she trembled inside with fear, she refused to show it as she took a step closer to him, standing inches from his nose. "We all know this was no accident and that you abused Jordan for your entire marriage."

Henry snorted. "And who do you think the jury will believe? A job-hopping barista or me, Jordan's successful, wealthy husband, who is now a CEO of a large software company?" He put an emphasis on the word 'wealthy' as though reminding her he could bribe his way to innocence.

No. She would find a way. She had to.

Sure, being a barista was not her ideal career, but it paid the bills. Her sister had offered to lend her money before she died, but Adriana had been too prideful to admit defeat. The truth was that Adriana had no idea what she wanted to do with her life, while her sister had been the wealthy owner of a software company. If their parents were alive, she was sure they would be prouder of Jordan, and Adriana wouldn't blame them.

But they were all gone now—Adriana's parents had died a few years ago when she and Jordan had been in their early twenties. All she had left was Megan.

And all Megan had was Adriana.

"And yes, in case you are wondering, I inherited everything, according to Jordan's will. Here, take a look if you want to." Henry thrust the paper toward Adriana, and her eyes skimmed over it, stating that Henry did indeed inherit the software company, the estate…and custody of Megan.

She shoved the paper back to him. "Let me take Megan home with me. You and I both know you don't really want her here. We'll all be happier if she's with me."

"No. She stays here."

"Why?" Adriana and Megan both demanded.

"Right now, I have custody of her. As I said, there's no way the court would grant custody to you over me. If you take her now, I'll call the police and tell them you kidnapped her."

Of course. Just as she'd expected. Adriana turned to Megan. "You and I will be together soon," she said with determination.

"Don't leave me!" Megan cried, running to her aunt and clinging to her.

Henry pried Megan's hands off Adriana. "Let her go, Megan." He looked at Adriana. "I want you out of here."

"It's okay, Megan. I'll come back for you soon," Adriana promised, then was instantly struck by guilt. What right did she have to make such a promise? Henry was right. Adriana had no chance in court against him.

She had no idea how she'd prove him guilty. But it was one promise she knew she would keep.

Adriana would find the evidence to prove Henry guilty, if it truly was the last thing she did on this earth.

"Out!" Henry cried, roughly grabbing Adriana's arm and dragging her out of Megan's room. He slammed the door, and Megan's cries resounded from the other side, cutting into Adriana's heart like shards of glass.

Adriana shoved Henry away from her as they walked. "Fine, I will leave." She stopped walking in the hallway and turned to face him once more. "I swear, if you harm her at all, I will make you pay."

Henry gave her a hard stare. "Get out of my house and don't come back, or I'll make Megan's life a nightmare, starting with boarding school." He pointed to the door.

How could she not come back and see Megan?

Adriana could still hear Megan crying as she hurried down the stairs. It broke her heart, and tears stung her eyes. She hated leaving her niece here with her monster of a stepfather, but she had no choice. She knew Henry truly would make Megan's life miserable if she didn't leave now. Would he really send her away to boarding school?

She didn't doubt it.

On her way out the door, Mrs. Clement followed Adriana, shutting the door behind them.

"Henry just told me to never come back or he'd send Megan away to boarding school," Adriana told the housekeeper, throwing her hands up. "I hate leaving her."

"Adriana, I must tell you something. I just overheard Henry on the phone with his lawyer right before he went upstairs and made you leave. All he talked about is that he is inheriting everything and that he is taking over the software company."

"I know. He just showed me the will."

"But that's the old version. He made Jordan make that will. But I know Jordan had a more recent will she made in secret, that states that you inherit everything and are in charge of it until Megan is older. It also says you have custody of Megan."

Adriana's head hurt, but her heart was filled with hope. "Really?" She put a hand to her temple, trying to absorb the news.

"Yes. She used a different lawyer because she didn't trust Henry or his lawyer. She thought she could trust him, but I think Henry found him and got to him. Henry must have paid his lawyer to use the older will, which states he gets everything. But I was there to witness and sign the new will the day Jordan had it made, and I know she has copies hidden away somewhere, just in case. She suspected Henry would do something like this. That's why she used a different lawyer. Here." Mrs. Clement pressed a business card into Adriana's hand. It read, *George Houser, Attorney at Law.* "Give him a call. He has a copy of the new will. Henry probably bribed or threatened him to say there is no new will and that Jordan never hired him, but maybe he will still help you. It's worth a try. I will also contact him."

14

Her head spinning, Adriana put a hand to her head, as if trying to stop her brain from somersaulting. "She left everything to me?"

"Well, yes, and to Megan. When she is older, she will have access, and until then, you will be in charge of everything—the software company, the estate, the money, and custody of Megan. But I don't have any idea where she hid the new will."

"Henry must hate me more than ever."

Adriana shivered, but it wasn't from the cold. *How far will he go to get rid of me?*

"You need to be careful, Adriana. Don't underestimate him. Maybe you should leave town," the housekeeper said, as if reading her thoughts.

"No, Megan needs me nearby. I can't leave her. Besides, I don't have any money right now."

"I can take care of her. I'm worried about your life, Adriana. If you're out of the picture, then he really would inherit everything. I can lend you money, if you need."

"Thank you, Mrs. Clement, especially for watching over Megan, but that won't be necessary. I'm not going anywhere," Adriana said adamantly. "I need to find evidence to prove that Henry killed my sister." She gave her friend a quick hug.

"I have faith you will," Mrs. Clement said.

As Adriana walked to her car, she looked up to Megan's window. Adriana waved, and Megan waved back.

"I promise, Megan. I'll find the evidence, then we will be together soon. Nothing will stop me," Adriana whispered.

CHAPTER TWO

Dominic Kauffman mucked his horse's stall at the back of his barn, whistling a tune. The sun wasn't even up yet, but he had always been a morning person. But these days, he often got up early for other reasons.

Last night, like many nights, he couldn't sleep. Nightmares had assailed him when he had dozed off, and he'd given up on sleep around four in the morning. When he was out here, with the horses, he got lost in his work and felt at peace.

"Dominic?" Damaris, his sister, called.

"I'm at the back of the barn, Damaris!"

Less than a minute later, his younger sister came into view. She was wearing a long brown dress, an apron tied over the front. Her brown hair was held back in a bun and covered by her *prayer kapp*, although there were a few stray strands. Dominic chuckled.

"What is so funny?" she asked.

"You have a little flour on your cheek," he said, pointing and smiling.

She brushed it away. "I was baking biscuits for breakfast." Damaris paused, looking at him thoughtfully. "You couldn't sleep again, could you? Did you have nightmares?"

She knew him too well.

Dominic set his shovel down and looked at his sister. "Is there something that you have to say, Damaris? You were obviously looking for me for a reason."

"Well..." she started hesitantly, and he remained quiet, his silence urging her to continue. "So, you see, I was talking with Margaret yesterday when I went to deliver bread to her mother."

This wouldn't be good.

"And...?" Dominic asked, even though he knew he was not going to like what his sister had to say next. He started shoveling again with ferocity.

"Well... She would really like to go to the Singing with you, and—"

"Why is she in such a hurry? Why doesn't she wait to be asked out to the Singing instead of talking about it with everyone?" Dominic interrupted his sister.

Her eyes lit up and she asked quickly, "So, you were going to ask her?"

"No, Damaris. I have no plans of courting Margaret, so of course I wasn't going to invite her to the Singing. Doing that would only be giving her the wrong impression. So do tell your friend to stop hoping." Dominic thrust his shovel into the manure with much more force than necessary.

"But she really likes you," Damaris argued.

"But I don't like her in that way. I heard that Mark asked to court her and she turned him down. I hope it wasn't because of me."

"Margaret is a really nice young lady, and she's pretty. Why don't you like her?"

"I know she's a great person, but I have no interest in marrying her. So, please stop playing matchmaker," Dominic said firmly.

Damaris huffed and said, "I told her that there was no point and it would be a waste of time, but she told me I should still try. I told her with you, there is no hope. You have no plans to ever get married again, do you?"

17

He stopped shoveling.

"Damaris..." Dominic said with a warning glance, and it stopped her spiel.

"I'm sorry," she said quietly. She whipped around, her dress billowing as she walked away. She stopped in her stride and turned around, causing Dominic to groan. She was obviously not done with all she had to say yet. "You should open up your heart and give love a chance again."

Dominic growled in frustration. What did she know about it? She hadn't had the person she'd loved the most ripped away from her. Damaris was young and naïve—she didn't understand true loss, but that wasn't her fault. Dominic knew his sister cared about him, but she had a funny way of showing it.

***

Adriana squinted in the assaulting wind, her face stinging as particles of ice blew in the dark. She clutched her knitted scarf tighter around her in a vain attempt to stay warm. A strong gust of wind chilled her as she hurried down the busy sidewalk of Portland, Maine, on her way home from work. The scent of saltwater from the nearby ocean hung in the air as she walked past a gelato shop.

Dejected, Adriana stared at the cobble-stone sidewalk as she trudged through the frigid weather. In one hand she held a coffee and a small paper bag with a bagel in it that she planned on eating in her car. In her other hand she held a shiny, red apple, and she bit into the fruit.

After seeing Jordan's lawyer, Mr. Houser, earlier that morning, she'd felt so hopeless.

"I don't know what you're talking about," Mr. Houser said when Adriana had asked him about the will Jordan had allegedly updated with him. "Jordan Phillips never contacted me about her will. She's not one of my clients."

"But her housekeeper, Mrs. Clement, said she was there and she signed it as a witness. Did Henry contact you? Is that why you won't tell me about Jordan's will?" Adriana persisted.

"You must be mistaken, Ms. Daniels. Your sister did not make or update her will with me. I'm sorry I can't be of more help," the lawyer said. "Is there anything else I can help you with?"

When Adriana asked about getting custody of Megan, the lawyer had told her she couldn't get custody of Megan unless a new will was found or her step-father, Henry, was proven unfit. And, of course, there was no evidence of that despite Adriana's belief he murdered her sister. How could she find proof?

"But I know you have a copy of the new will!" Adriana snapped. "Or...you *had* one."

She took a deep breath and lowered her voice when other people in the office looked at her. Obviously, this man was too afraid to give her the new will. "Henry is a manipulative, intimidating person. I'm sorry he got to you. I'll find another way. Thank you, Mr. Houser."

She left the firm and went to the police to report that the will Henry had was the older version, and that there was a new one stating she had inherited everything. But the police captain had told her that was just hearsay and that she had no evidence, even warning her not to make such serious accusations without evidence or it could result in civil liability for slander, or she could be charged for wasting police time by making a false report. On her way out of his office, she couldn't help but notice the photograph of the police captain and Henry on the wall at some social gathering.

Was he in Henry's pocket, too?

Right now, all she could do was find the new will. Going to Jordan's house and aggravating Henry wouldn't help her case. Even if she went when he wasn't home, she suspected he had security cameras on his property. He might even report her for breaking and entering, and she had no doubt the police would believe him.

Adriana shook her head in frustration. Why didn't Henry just let Megan stay with her? What did he want her there for? It wasn't like he even loved her at all.

Adriana turned down a side street, shivering, but it wasn't from the cold. She hated this part of town, especially at night. She took another bite of the apple, pulling her scarf tighter around her.

She heard footsteps behind her. Her hearing dulled against the sound of her own pulse. Panic shot through her as she looked over her shoulder, quickening her steps. No one was there, so she kept walking. Maybe her paranoia was making her hear things. Or it could have been a rat.

She slowed when she saw someone hunkered down, their face hidden by a tattered hooded sweatshirt. It was common to see homeless people in this city, but Adriana's compassion for them never lessened. She'd seen this man outside the coffee shop where she worked, and many times she'd brought out hot coffee to him. She'd come to expect his visits, though the only words he'd uttered to her had been "thank you."

Now, the man looked freezing. What could she do to help him?

"Hi, there," Adriana said, bending down to his level and removing the knitted scarf from her neck. "Good to see you again. Please, take this."

The man slowly lifted his head to look at her. Adriana shrank back when she thought she saw evil in his eyes for a split second, and she almost ran. Then the look in his eyes melted away, revealing confusion.

"You're…giving this to me?" he asked in a scratchy voice.

"Of course. And take this, too," she said, handing him a paper bag with a bagel in it from the coffee shop and a hot coffee she hadn't sipped yet. "It's not much, but it'll fill you up for a little while."

The man just looked at her, completely befuddled. "Thank you, ma'am."

"May I pray for you, sir?" Adriana asked. Sure, it might be considered out of the ordinary to pray for a stranger, but she felt a connection to this man, and she knew in her heart that the Holy Spirit was asking her to do this now, and she wanted to do what was right.

"Pray for me?" the man asked, scratching his chin in bewilderment. "No one has ever done that for me."

"Let me be the first," Adriana said. "You know, I've brought you coffee outside the shop a few times now, but you never told me your name. So, what's your name?"

He hesitated. "Bill."

"Dear Lord," she said, bowing her head. She didn't close her eyes, just so she could watch what was going on around her on the dark street, always staying alert. "Please watch over Bill. I don't know his struggles, but you do. Please be with him, keep him safe, and keep him warm. You see when a sparrow falls, so surely you see what could be troubling Bill. Please be with him. Amen."

When Adriana looked up, Bill's eyes were filled with tears. He stood up so suddenly, Adriana jerked back and shot away from him in case she had to protect herself.

"I can't do this," Bill said, pacing, and that was when she noticed how his hand was gripping something at his side, hidden underneath his coat.

Was that a...knife? She took several quick steps back.

"You have to get away from here, Adriana," Bill whispered. "Right now."

Realization and dread crept into Adriana's veins, and she halted. "How do you know my name? Have you been following me?"

"Yes. I was hired to kill you and make it look like a homeless man mugged you and murdered you. But I know now there is no way I can do that, not after how kind you've been to me at the coffee shop and here now," Bill said, his words rushing out so quickly, Adriana could hardly grasp them. "You're the kindest person I've ever met. What you just did for me, a stranger... No one has ever done anything like that for me before."

"Who hired you?" Adriana demanded, but she already knew the answer.

"I think you know. You have to run. Get as far away from here as you can," Bill urged her, waving his arms. "I'll tell him I killed you, but that won't buy you much time. He will figure it out eventually. He hired me to cut out your heart and bring it to him."

Adriana set her hand on her chest, sickness filling her stomach. "My…heart?" She knew Henry was twisted and psychotic, but she had no idea how much until now.

"Yes. He wants you dead, and he will stop at nothing. You have to go." When she hesitated, the assassin roared, "Go!"

Adriana whirled around and bolted down the street, running to her car, ignoring the biting snow whipping against her face. As she turned, she dropped the apple, leaving the forgotten fruit in the snow.

Where would she go? What would she do? She had no money, and she couldn't leave the country. All she could do was get in her car and drive away as fast as she could until her gas money ran out.

But what about Megan? She couldn't just leave her behind.

She had to go get her first and take Megan with her, even if Henry did call the police on her for kidnapping.

Adriana reached her car and started it, rubbing her hands together, trying to get some warmth into her bones.

Just then her phone rang in her pocket, and she jumped. The screen said Mrs. Clement's name.

"Hello?" Adriana's voice cracked with emotion. Right now, hearing Mrs. Clement's voice was what she needed most of all.

"Adriana," Mrs. Clement said, "You sound scared. Are you okay?"

"God knew I needed to hear your voice right now." Adriana quickly explained what happened. "I have to come get Megan. Is she there?" Adriana demanded, staring straight ahead at the swirling snow.

"She's here. But you can't take her," Mrs. Clement said. "Remember? He will tell the authorities you kidnapped her, and it would be believable. You'll never get custody of her."

"She's not safe with him! Especially after what just happened."

"You're no good to her in jail. I'll watch over her, Adriana. Right now, you have to get away, or you'll be dead. At least until we find the new will. You have to leave right now. Do you have enough money for gas right now?"

"Not much. I can maybe drive a few hours."

"Hide out somewhere for a while until we can figure out what to do," Mrs. Clement said. "Then, after the will is found and you have custody of Megan, you can come back for her. You could even leave the country with her if you want. With that kind of money, you can go anywhere you want."

"We won't have to leave the country to get away from him. I'll prove he killed my sister," Adriana said breathlessly, still in shock. "Please let Megan know I love her."

"I will. I will do my absolute best to keep her safe," Mrs. Clement said, and Adriana swelled with gratitude.

"Thank you. Please call me if you need anything. I don't know what I'd do without you."

"Right now, you've got to go. Goodbye, Adriana. See you soon."

The phone disconnected, and Adriana sped away, not even knowing where she was going.

"Lord, please be with Megan. I know she's probably scared and confused. Please let me live long enough to make sure she's safe," Adriana prayed.

She drove through a small town, then down a long road surrounded by fields that seemed never-ending. She passed a yellow, diamond-shaped sign with an image of a horse and buggy on it.

Did Amish live in this area? She had no idea there were Amish in Maine.

Adriana lifted her foot off the gas when a buggy came into view. She wanted to give it plenty of room and drive by it slowly.

Panic caused her heart to trip as she stepped on the brake, but the car refused to respond. Her car kept on speeding ahead.

"Lord, help me!" Adriana screamed as she continued to stomp on the brake, but still, her car would not stop. Another car was approaching on the opposite side of the road, and if she didn't slow down right now, she feared she would hit either the car or the buggy head-on.

Was this Henry's doing? After the assassin failed, had he hired someone to cut her brakes?

As her car came closer to the buggy and the other vehicle, Adriana had a choice to make.

She swerved her car out of the way of the buggy and vehicle before they could collide, opened her car door, and leapt out into the snow.

***

CHAPTER THREE

As Dominic was feeding the horses, a loud crash sounded in the distance. He ran out of the barn and looked up to see billowing smoke rising near the Willows' farm. Dominic dashed back into the barn and led his horse, Apple, out.

Damaris ran out of the barn after him. "Dominic! What are you doing?"

As he climbed onto the horse, he said, "Stay here. I'll go see what happened."

"Brother, don't be so reckless. It could be dangerous!" she called.

"We have no idea who is hurt. Please, for once, listen to me. Tell Danny to find me near the Willows' farm and to bring the buggy!" Dominic called. Ignoring his sister's frustrated groan, he cantered off, headed towards the rising black smoke.

Dominic and Apple raced across the snowy landscape. He shivered in the frigid cold as the wind whipped past him. The fire was not at the Willows' farm, but it was near there. It was just at the edge of the woods that bordered the eastern end of the little Amish community. Dominic dismounted Apple and approached the scene carefully.

A car had crashed into a tree. Flames licked the car, but Dominic got just close enough to see inside. As soon as he set his eyes on it, they narrowed. Where was the driver?

Visions of seeing his wife killed right in front of him flooded his mind, the blood dripping from her face and hair...

"Focus," Dominic muttered, mentally kicking himself to rid his mind of the memories. Now was not the time to regret his past and wish things were different. He was here to find the victim of this car crash—or find the body.

He bent low as he searched around the car. The car had been burned beyond recognition. What could have caused such damage? It certainly could not have been because it careened into a tree or something related to an accident. The car was too damaged for that. It was as if someone had put explosives in the car. Perhaps to cover up evidence?

"Dominic!"

Dominic looked up to see Sid Hoffman, his neighbor, running down the incline toward him.

"I was driving my buggy," the elderly Amish man said, trying to catch his breath. "Another car was coming, and this car veered right off the road behind me without stopping or slowing down. What happened?"

"I'm not sure," Dominic said. "Something isn't right." Dominic looked down the road, realizing there were no brake marks. Yes, something definitely wasn't right.

"I think I saw her jump out of the car before it crashed," Sid said.

"Let's go find her."

He swallowed. He had to search fast. There could be someone out there who was injured or, worse still, bleeding to death, or possibly with burn injuries. The temperature was dropping fast. If they weren't found tonight, they could freeze out here.

However, he could not help but wonder if someone could have survived being flung out of that vehicle.

Still, he had to try.

"I'll go search over there," Sid said, then hurried off in the other direction.

Dominic walked Apple along the edge of the road and watched the road as cars flew by. Just then, Apple's ears pinned back, his eyes darting.

"What is it, boy?" Dominic whispered. "Did you hear something?"

There. What was that?

Dominic heard a faint whimper, and his head shot up. He looked around. Where had it come from? He heard it again and followed it.

He found the source. Down a small incline near the road, partially covered by bushes, lay a person.

"Sid!" Dominic called out. "I found her!"

From the person's long dark hair, Dominic guessed it was a girl or a woman, and it appeared as though she'd rolled down from the road and had been stopped by the bushes. It was fortunate that she was not right beside the road or she might have been crushed by an oncoming vehicle.

Dominic swallowed hard as he hurried to her while carefully leading Apple down the incline. A bitter taste formed in his mouth as he realized how the bushes concealed her. If not for that whimper and Apple's sharp ears, he might not have found her.

He released Apple's reins and turned the person over. His eyes widened. It was indeed a young woman, barely conscious. Her pale face was caked with dirt from where she had been lying. Her dark hair surrounded her head, flowing onto the snow. Her dark eyelashes stood out against her light skin. Blood trickled down her face from a gash in her head and stained her hair, making it sticky to the touch.

Dominic placed his fingers on her wrist. She still had a pulse, but it was weak, barely noticeable.

He looked her over, wondering if anything was broken. She was wearing a white turtleneck sweater, black jeans, and matching black boots. The sweater was stained with blood and dirt. Dominic pulled off the scarf around his neck and used it to apply pressure around her head, hoping it would stop the bleeding.

Her white sweater was still pooling with blood. She had to be bleeding from somewhere other than her head. He lifted the edge of her shirt, looking for the second injury, and took in a sharp breath when he saw a cut on her abdomen. It was bleeding but didn't look very deep. Hopefully, it would be fine with some stitches.

Who was she and what had she gotten herself involved in?

Dominic's younger teenage brother, Danny, drove over to them in a buggy as Sid hobbled over.

Danny hopped out and ran forward, his brown hair covered by a straw hat. His eyes widened when he saw the injured woman, and he took Apple's reins.

"What happened, Dominic?" Danny asked. "This doesn't look good."

"Do you think she will be all right?" Sid asked.

"She is hurt," Dominic said. As he carried her over to the buggy and settled her inside.

Dominic turned to look at his brother and motioned towards the other side of the community. "Take Apple and go call an ambulance. She needs to get to the hospital."

The woman in his arms finally stirred. "No… No," she stammered in a cracking voice. "No hospital."

Sid gave Dominic a questioning glance.

"Ma'am, you need to go to the hospital," Dominic urged.

"No," her voice trailed off before she slipped back   into unconsciousness. "He'll find me… He'll kill me…"

Dominic, Sid, and Danny looked at each other in confusion.

Dominic shook his head. "Someone must be after her. Maybe that's why she doesn't want to go to the hospital. It might be one of the first places they'll look for her. I'm guessing she doesn't want the police to find her either. Danny, take Apple and go to the phone shanty to call Doctor McAllister. Go as fast as you can. We can trust him to be discreet."

Danny put his hands on his hips. "But, Dominic, she needs the hospital—"

"No. You heard her. Go call the doctor." Every minute they delayed drew the young woman closer to death's door. They had to try what they could to see if she could be healed and when all that failed, only then would he accept that it was God's will for her. "Doctor McAllister can be trusted."

"Oh, fine," Danny said. Though he was often grumpy, the boy had a good heart. "If you say so." He galloped away.

"Is there anything I can do?" Sid asked.

"For now, go home, but please do not tell anyone except your wife about this. It's for her own safety. I have a feeling someone is after her, so we should be discreet," Dominic said.

"Of course. Let me know if I can do anything," Sid said, then returned to his buggy.

Sirens sounded in the distance.

Dominic climbed onto the buggy that Danny had brought and started a slow and careful ride home.

CHAPTER FOUR

"Well, what can you tell me, Doctor?" Dominic asked Doctor McAllister. The doctor was a non-Amish man who lived down the street and had succeeded in getting the trust of the Amish people. Sometimes they went to him, and in some cases like this, he came to them.

He was an elderly man with a spattering of silvery white hair, a matching moustache and a tall build. But even with his height, he still had to look up at Dominic while he spoke. Night had already fallen, and he had spent all of the afternoon with the hurt woman.

The doctor shook his head and said, "That young woman is very lucky both in surviving the accident and in how you found her. However, I am inclined to believe she was not directly involved in the accident."

"What do you mean, Doctor?" Dominic asked as he crossed his arms, his eyes searching the fields for signs of any animals that had not been taken into the barn for the night.

"You see, if she was flung out of the car because of the force, she would have lots of broken bones. But she only has a sprained ankle, a cut on her abdomen, and the gash in her head, which worries me a lot, if I do say so myself."

"So, what do you think?"

"As an emergency doctor for over twenty years, I have seen many accident victims. From how you've described the car, I do not believe that it was just an accident. This should be investigated."

"It can't, Doctor. We cannot bring in the police to investigate, not yet, for the woman's safety. Besides, you know the Amish way," Dominic said pointedly, and the doctor nodded.

"You said she didn't want to go to the hospital, afraid someone would find her. Don't you think that her life is in danger?"

"We cannot know that for sure until she wakes. And it is more reason why we cannot let anyone outside know what is happening. We have no idea what happened," Dominic argued. "We don't know if it was an accident or if someone was trying to kill her."

Despite the situation, the doctor chuckled and said, "Oh, Dominic, you are a smart young man, and I forget most times that there is no arguing with you. Indeed, law enforcement could use a man with innate instincts like yours."

Ignoring the last bit of the doctor's statement, Dominic walked down the road with the doctor. "Thank you for driving here so quickly tonight, but from now on, Danny or I will be coming to pick you up in the buggy. We can't draw attention to you driving in and out of the community. I can trust my community to keep this issue hidden, but out there, I don't know who can be trusted. Now, how is she doing?"

The doctor nodded. "I was able to stitch up the small cut on her abdomen, but like I told you, my worry stems from the wound on her head. She obviously made impact with something, and we will not know the effect until she wakes. There could potentially be memory loss or internal bleeding. The next few days are crucial. Keep that in mind."

"I understand," Dominic said quietly as they stepped outside. "But I believe that God is in control. She was able to get out of a car careening toward the woods. I am more than sure she will be able to survive this. The good Lord will keep her. Good night, Doctor. Thank you."

"I'll come see her tomorrow," the doctor agreed as he climbed into his car.

As the car's tires kicked up dust in the driveway, Dominic tapped his chin thoughtfully. He turned around to go into the house when he heard his name being called. He knew the voice, and he sighed as he turned around.

Margaret walked down the driveway toward him.

Dominic groaned inwardly. She'd seen the doctor, and now she'd ask questions.

Her red hair shone in the sunlight, and her green eyes studied him under dark lashes. She was indeed beautiful, but Dominic knew he would never have romantic feelings for her. They'd been friends their entire lives, and he wanted it to remain that way. She deserved a man who loved her, and Dominic was not that man.

"Good evening, Margaret," he said.

She smiled and said, "Good evening, Dominic. Was that Doctor McAllister leaving? Is everyone okay?"

"Everyone is fine, Margaret. We just have a guest who is not feeling too well," he said quietly. "Please. I trust that you will be discreet." It was a statement, but he said it more like a question.

"Oh, I see," she said as she wrinkled her nose. "Who is it?"

Dodging her question, he said, "Everything is fine, really. Please, we would appreciate it if you didn't tell anyone. Actually, we have a lot to do, so now isn't a good time. I'll let Damaris know you stopped by. Good day," he said, hurrying into the house and closing the door, despite her trying to get a word in.

Not waiting for her to say anything else, Dominic headed to the bedroom where the woman was staying and stood by the door as he watched his mother, Constance, clean the young woman's face in the light of the propane light on the ceiling.

She looked up just then and shook her head, dropping the cloth in the bowl of water. She clasped her hands together and said, "Who would do such a thing to a fellow human being? It is terrible. The world is full of so much evil. What did the doctor say?"

Dominic shrugged, still leaning on the doorpost. "We won't know how she is really doing until she wakes up. So all we can do is wait."

His mother shook her head and said, "I believe she will be well. The good Lord made it possible for you to find her so she can get well here."

"Yes, I believe He did, Mother," Dominic said as he looked from his mother back to the woman. No longer was she wearing the stained top, pants, or boots. His mother had changed her clothes and now she had on a gray Amish dress. Her hair had been cleaned, and he could now see that indeed it actually was dark brown, almost black.

His mother sighed, and Dominic hurried forward and placed a hand on his mother's shoulder.

"Go on and get some rest, Mother. I am sure it was a busy day at the market, and Damaris could probably use help with the children. I will sit here through the night. You should not need to stress yourself. I doubt she will be waking up tonight."

"Thank you, son," she said. She smiled at him as she stood up and tapped his cheek lightly. She looked back to the young woman on the bed and back to him. "Good night. Tomorrow is another day. I hope it is brighter for you than today was."

Dominic sighed as his mother left. Every night ever since he returned to the community three years ago, she told him that before going to bed. She kept hoping and believing that someday the cloud of darkness would leave his eyes. Dominic sat at the side of the bed, wishing as he did every night that his mother's prayer was answered.

Dominic stared hard at the woman, and for the first time, with the dirt and the blood out of the way, he really saw her face. Her dark eyelashes rested on her cheeks and as he watched, they kept quivering. It was like she was trying desperately to open them but not having luck. Her mouth was slightly open, and as he studied her, he saw that she was beautiful. She had a certain tranquility about her, and he could not understand why someone would want to hurt her.

Before his eyes, her mouth started moving slowly. If he had not been looking so hard, he would not have seen it. He closed the gap between them and placed his ear close to her mouth.

"Jordan… Megan…," she kept saying over and over again.

What had happened to her? Who were Jordan and Megan?

Dominic placed his hand on her forehead and felt that her temperature was rising. Sighing, he placed the cold washcloth back on her head. It was going to be a long night; he knew that for sure.

***

Another morning met Dominic sitting in a hard-back chair at the side of the bed. It was one he had constructed with his own hands. In fact, the entire house and the furniture within were borne of the work of his hands. He had dedicated sweat and time into raising the house, and members of the community had helped too. But the furniture, from the beds to the smallest stool, had all been handmade by him or his father.

It was the second morning dawning since he had brought the hurt woman to the house. Two nights had passed already, and she still had a temperature, and she was still very much unconscious. Sid had come by to see how she was doing a few times.

The doctor said to continue monitoring her and keeping her temperature down, but more would have to be done if she did not wake to eat and drink soon.

Dominic woke up to the smell of baking bread. He sat up and his eyes immediately flitted over to the woman on the bed. She looked just the same as the previous day and the night, although she seemed calmer. At least she was no longer talking in her sleep like she had done throughout the previous day after the first night. He reached out and placed his hand on her forehead. She still had a temperature, but compared to the previous day, it was better.

He stood up and stretched out. He had to tend the farm and the animals.

Dominic looked back at the mysterious woman for one last time before he headed out of the room, through the house and to the kitchen. It had large windows which he had constructed to let lots of light into the house. His mother had always said that the kitchen should be the cheeriest part of the house. He walked in to find his mother at the counter.

"Good morning, *Maam*," he said, walking up to her and giving her a hug. She smiled up at him and patted his shoulder. Gone were the days that she could pat his head. He had grown much taller than her.

"Good morning, son," she looked closely at him and smiled ruefully. Dominic knew what was going through her head. She always gave him that look of perusal every morning. He knew she would never stop praying. She would keep hoping for the light to return to his eyes. "I believe you slept well. How did our guest do last night?"

"Restless all through," he said quietly. At this, his mother looked up from the freshly baked bread she was slicing.

"What happened?"

"She kept talking in her sleep like she did throughout yesterday, repeating the names Jordan and Megan." He sighed. "Doctor McAllister did say these first couple of days are critical."

"I see... Well, I'm going to prepare my honey and lemon balm later in the day. I should have done it yesterday. It will help with the fever and her restlessness. And you also know how effective it is. It is the perfect medicine for everything."

"Considering how much you gave to Dominic, too bad it could not cure a broken heart," Damaris said, strolling into the kitchen.

Dominic rolled his eyes.

"So, who is this mystery woman and what are we going to do with her?" Damaris asked.

"No one can know," Dominic said as he walked out of the kitchen, his sister fast behind him. "Not yet. Not until we know more."

"Tell me. Who is she?" Damaris asked as they stepped out of the house through the back door. "Do you even know?"

Dominic looked at his sister and pulled on his hat, which had been hanging on a stand just in the hall leading to the back door. "Not yet."

As they walked towards the barn, Damaris followed closely behind him. "But who is she? Tongues have already started wagging, brother. You know the police have asked some families if they know anything about the car crash, starting with the Willows."

"Are people saying anything to the police?" Dominic asked as he opened the pen, letting the cattle out into the fields.

"No, of course not. You know it is against our ways to answer questions from the police. But some are gossiping amongst themselves, saying you brought an outsider in, and that she's in trouble."

"She has been here two nights and the rumor mill is already on fire? They don't know her situation. I still think someone is after her, so that's why I didn't take her to the hospital. She asked me not to. Was I supposed to leave her to bleed to death? Aren't we to love each other and our neighbors as ourselves?" Dominic asked as they gave the horses hay.

"Some say you actually knew who she was before you brought her in, that you were romantically involved with her," Damaris said.

"Preposterous!" People gobbled up juicy gossip, especially in a small village like theirs where there was barely anything new to talk about. Dominic's brown eyes flashed and he said, "Clearly they don't know she's unconscious. People always enjoy digging into my life, especially when it has to do with romance and marriage."

"Can you blame them? After what happened with..." Damaris stopped when Dominic gave her a look.

"I never saw this woman until two days ago," Dominic said quietly. "She hasn't even woken up yet."

"I know that, but—"

A scream tore through the air, and their heads swiveled in the direction of the house.

CHAPTER FIVE

Dominic entered the room and found his mother sitting beside the woman, trying to calm her down. She was sitting up and was holding the sheet around her tightly, gasping for air.

"You are safe, child. This is a place of love. No one is going to hurt you here," Constance said.

Dominic's entrance caused the woman's eyes to fly in his direction. As soon as her gaze met his, Dominic froze. Her eyes were the darkest shade of green he had ever seen, and there were gold flecks within them, but that was not what pulled at his heartstrings.

No. It was the haunted look that lay within them.

"Where am I?" she asked.

As he stepped forward slowly, his mother stood up and let him sit. His eyes never left hers, and he saw that hers never left his either.

He settled himself beside her and said, "You are in an Amish community in Unity, Maine. You were involved in an accident, and I found you. Do you know what you were doing around this area?"

"Unity?" she asked, and he nodded. She shook her head slowly, looked at his mother, then back at him.

"Does that sound familiar?" Dominic asked.

"I...I don't know."

"Okay, why don't we start out easy then? What is your name?" Dominic asked her, smiling reassuringly.

She looked at him and then her eyes widened as they became moist. Her hands raked through her hair. "What's my name? I...I don't know my name."

Dominic moved forward, taking her hand in his. She flinched at first, then relaxed, gripping his hand tightly.

His mother's hands were clasped in prayer.

"Call Doctor McAllister now, please, *Maam*."

His mother did not hesitate and was out the door in a flash.

"You'll be okay," Dominic kept telling the woman.

***

Where on earth am I? Adriana thought in a panic. Yes, she had lied about not remembering her name, but she had no idea where she was.

Her hand immediately went to her tiny gold key necklace, a gift from her sister.

Who was this man in pilgrim-like clothing?

All at once, images slammed together in her brain. Jordan's death, Megan crying...

And jumping out of her moving car.

Her brakes had stopped working. Henry must have had someone disable them. Knowing the car wouldn't stop until it crashed, she had to get out. The full weight of the situation crashing down on her had forced Adriana to open her door. She'd jumped out of the moving car, landing on the snow, then she'd rolled down a small slope. Only seconds later, the car had crashed into a tree.

That's where she'd seen this man before. He'd carried her to a buggy and brought her here.

"Miss? Are you okay? You must be so confused. You were in an accident. My name is Dominic. I found you and brought you here to take care of you. You said you didn't want to go to a hospital because someone might kill you. So I brought you here. The police have asked some families if they know anything, but don't worry. We Amish do not answer questions from the police or report crimes. You're safe here."

Relief flooded through her. She hadn't known that about the Amish, but she was grateful they were being discreet. "Thank you for bringing me here and not the hospital. I really appreciate that."

More than you know, she added silently. If he had taken her to the hospital, she was sure Henry would have found her by now.

"Do you remember the crash? Anything?" the kind young man, Dominic, asked.

She remembered all of it, though she wished she didn't.

Yet, she found herself shaking her head. As she looked over her body, seeing bandages and not having any idea how bad her injuries were, who knew how long she would be stuck here? How long would she be able to keep up a charade with a fake backstory? And if she slipped up, they might figure out who she was, and Henry might find her.

Not knowing what else to do, she stared down at the sheet covering her. The sounds of children playing came from downstairs and from the backyard. Out the window, fields rolled on for what looked like miles.

What was this place? Wherever she was, she couldn't endanger these people by revealing her name to them.

"No. I don't remember anything," she lied.

***

"Well, Doctor?" Dominic, Damaris, and their mother were seated in the kitchen with the doctor.

He set his cup of tea down and rubbed his hands together. "It's like I told you, Dominic. She is having trouble recollecting her memories. It's a case of amnesia, hopefully temporary. She's probably endured a lot of stress and trauma. Details about herself and her life are difficult for her to grasp. She is trying desperately to place the pieces together."

"How long is this going to last? I mean, she certainly can't stay here forever, but she can't leave if she doesn't know where to go to," Damaris said.

"It varies. Hard to say. Days, weeks, months, years… Some people never regain their memories, but hopefully, she will."

At this, Constance gasped and they all turned to her. Dominic stretched out a hand and touched his mother's shoulder.

"Mother, why don't you check on her? Now that she is awake and knows nothing, she must be scared and would appreciate some company."

Constance hurried off, and Dominic sighed. His mother had suffered so much loss and hearing such news was not helpful. He turned back to the doctor and asked, "What do we do, Doctor?"

"First things first. We need to treat the source of the memory loss and, in this case, it is the head trauma she suffered. I will be prescribing drugs for that. And then if it persists, treatment through therapy would help. It is good to show her familiar sights and smells and places, but it is impossible here. Above all, patience is key."

"And she will get better?" an impatient Damaris asked.

"That is the plan." The doctor stood up and rubbed his hands together. "I will be back later."

Dominic nodded at Damaris, urging her to see the doctor out. Once they were out the door, he stood up and headed back to the room. The woman was seated, and there was a wooden tray in front of her with soup and homemade bread. He could see his mother hovering like a hawk while the woman ate. She kept wringing her hands and tugging at her prayer *kapp,* and he knew his mother well enough to know that she was nervous.

He cleared his throat as he entered the room.

"Why don't you head to the market, *Maam*? You have those pie and bread deliveries to make. I can take it from here," he told her.

She shook her head nervously as she said, "If I leave you alone with her, it will only raise more brows."

"Mother, am I doing anything wrong?"

"No, but—"

"That is all there is to it, *Maam*. My heart and my hands are clean. Go on."

She nodded, then left. Dominic gestured to the chair by the door and looked at the woman questioningly.

"Can I sit?"

She nodded, setting the bowl of soup down. "Thank you for saving me."

He sat down. "You remember? You were drifting in and out of consciousness."

"Uh… No. Your mother told me about it," she said quietly. She looked up at him with soulful eyes and said, "Thank you."

Dominic nodded and said, "We have the Lord to thank. So, you have no idea what happened to you?"

"No, I don't." She shook her head. "Have you called the authorities?"

"Well... You see, this is an Amish community, and we do not report things to the police."

"And I heard someone mention you don't have telephones. I don't know if that's a good thing or a bad thing." She added the last part in a mutter, and Dominic looked at her inquisitively.

"Well, we have one in the community phone shanty down the lane, and most of the Amish businesses have them. We just don't have them in our homes."

"I might not remember my life, but I know with all affirmation that all this is new to me."

Dominic smiled and nodded. "Yes, I can confirm that. You were wearing non-Amish clothes and again, you were in a car so... I put that together already. But that's not the reason why I didn't call the police. I would have, even though it's against our ways, but you told me not to take you to the hospital. You said someone would find you. So, I figured I shouldn't report this either, in case someone really is looking for you. Do you remember who might be after you?"

The woman crossed her arms as she looked at him. She tried to adjust herself, but then she winced, and he stretched out a hand automatically to help her. He set the quilted feather pillows firmly behind her.

"Thanks." She smiled up at him as he hovered over her.

"Uh, sure." He cleared his throat and sat back on the side of the bed. "So, do you?"

She shook her head slowly. "No. I don't remember who is after me, but I have this terrible feeling that if you do report this to the police or if I did go to the hospital, I would be in danger. So, thank you."

"You're welcome. You're safe here."

"So... Was there anything on me? An ID or anything?" she probed.

Dominic shook his head. "There was nothing—not even a cellphone or purse. I bet they were in the car and burned. Do you remember who Jordan and Megan are?"

Adriana went still, wondering if the panic on her face was as obvious as it felt.

How did he know their names? What else did he know?

Since her phone had been burned in the crash, she'd have to find a phone and call Mrs. Clement to check on Megan as soon as she could walk.

He moved closer to her. "Do you?"

Adriana shook her head, trying to rein in her thoughts. "No, but that name has been resounding in my head since I woke up. I think I'm supposed to know who it is, but I just don't remember," she lied. "Why? How do you know those names?"

"You've been saying their names in your sleep. It's okay. Don't force it. It will come. Well, we don't know your name, but we need to call you something. What do you want us to call you?"

Adriana fell silent, then turned her head to look out the window at the swirling snow flurrying outside. Good question. What were they supposed to call her?

"How about Snow? I like the snow," she said, "And you found me in the snow." She tried not to wince at how bad of a liar she was, and how silly of a name that was, but Dominic didn't seem to notice.

Dominic grinned. "That's a great name. I like it. Snow it is."

Really? He bought that? she thought, tilting her head to the side as she watched him.

There was a sound at the door, and they looked up to see a young woman.

"This is my sister, Damaris," Dominic said. "Damaris, this is Snow."

"Snow?" Damaris asked in confusion.

"We are calling her that until she remembers her name."

"Ah. So, you're finally awake. When are you leaving?" Damaris asked, a hand on her hip.

Adriana lifted one eyebrow. "Hey, it's not like I want to be here, either. Sorry to impose," she said, then bit her lip, wishing the words hadn't come out so coldly.

"Damaris, let's go so we can talk," Dominic said quietly, picking up the food tray. He looked back at Adriana and smiled. "I'll be right back."

Fine with me, Adriana thought. She needed a minute to think.

***

Reluctantly, Dominic left the room.

"Snow is injured, Damaris. She will be staying with us a while longer," he said quietly as they made their way to the kitchen.

"Seriously? You're calling her Snow?"

"That's the name she picked, and I like it."

"Isn't she supposed to stay till she heals and then leave immediately?"

"Oh, come on, Damaris. You were raised better than that. We have been brought up to love our neighbors as ourselves, so why such hatred towards her?" Dominic set the tray on the counter. "She was just in an accident. She needs more time to heal."

"She is not a neighbor. She is a complete stranger. And I don't hate her, but if she had not been here, you would have come to the Singing with me two days ago," Damaris retorted.

"Now that is where you are wrong, Damaris. I already told you that I was not going to court Margaret, so I probably wouldn't have gone to the Singing anyway. Secondly, she might be a stranger, but were we all not put on this earth by the Lord?"

At that, his sister had nothing to say. She crossed her arms.

"When she gets better, she will leave. She didn't want us to take her to the hospital because she was afraid someone would find her. Her life could be in danger."

"Then she is endangering all of us!" Damaris cried, throwing her hands up.

"She is staying here. *Maam* and I have already decided."

Damaris let out a growl and stomped out of the room. Dominic sighed and returned to Snow's room.

His eyes widened when he didn't see her there. Where had she gone to? He panicked.

"Hi."

He heard a voice, and he swerved around to find her leaning against the door, pain written all over her face. He hurried over and helped her into the bed. "I needed to use the bathroom."

"Why didn't you call for help? Damaris could have helped."

She smiled at him and said, "Thanks. But I'm fine. I'm feeling much better, thank you."

"Would you like to meet my younger brothers and sisters?" Dominic asked.

"Oh, yes, I'd love to." Snow grinned.

"Let me go get them." Dominic left the room, and a moment later, he returned with all his other siblings.

"Oh, my!" Snow said, eyebrows raised. "You have six younger brothers and sisters, counting Damaris? There are seven of you?"

"Yes. There are seven of us, and I'm the oldest," Dominic said. "Damaris is the next oldest. This is Delphine, Danny, Dean, Daisy, and Desmond, oldest to youngest."

51

All of them stared at her.

"Are you sick?" Dean asked, then sneezed loudly.

"God bless you," Snow said.

"He has a lot of allergies. Are we adopting you?" Daisy asked, bouncing on her toes and teetering off balance. "Forever and ever and ever?"

"Oh, come on. We are not adopting her," Danny said gruffly, crossing his arms and rolling his eyes. "She's an adult."

Desmond asked something in another language, rubbing his eyes.

"What did he say?" Snow asked Dominic.

"He hasn't learned much English yet," Dominic said. "The children learn Pennsylvania Dutch first, then English. He asked if you always sleep so much, and he said he likes to sleep too."

"Oh," Snow said with a laugh. "No, I don't always sleep this much. It is only because I got hurt."

Delphine just smiled at her, hiding behind Dominic's leg.

"She's a bit shy sometimes," Dominic said to Snow.

Snow laughed, and Dominic was grateful she didn't seem overwhelmed. "I'm not sick," she explained to the children. "I just bumped my head. Dominic rescued me and is taking good care of me. Once I figure out who my family is, I'll have to go home."

"Well, kids, why don't you go play so we can let Snow rest?" Dominic said, ushering them out the door.

"It was nice to meet you all!" Snow called.

"Nice to meet you, too," Daisy said, grinning at her. "I'm happy you're here."

"Why, thank you, Daisy," Snow said. She looked to Dominic as the children left the room. "I don't need rest, Dominic. I've been sleeping for what seems like weeks."

"Well, how about a game of cards instead?" Dominic asked, mischief in his eyes.

"That sounds wonderful."

"I could teach you how to play Solitaire, but it's a game for one person. I also know a more fun, fast-paced card game called Dutch Blitz. Would you rather have a slow-paced game or a more fast-paced game?"

"Dutch Blitz sounds more fun. And I could use a little fun. Might help ease my mind."

As he taught her how to play, they took a break between rounds.

"You weren't kidding. That is fast-paced," she said, laughing. "My brain needs a minute to catch up." Snow looked at him thoughtfully. "Where did you get that scar on your forehead? Were you in an accident too?"

Dominic's hand subconsciously went to cover the scar. Visions of bright headlights racing toward his car at an unimaginable speed filled his mind.

"Yes," he murmured. "I was in a car accident, too, like you. That was when I left the Amish for a few years, but I came back after that."

"You're blessed. You survived. God protected you."

Although he knew the words were supposed to comfort him, they angered him, just like every other time he'd heard them from his friends.

In his mind, he saw the drunk driver's truck heading right toward his wife's side of the car, who'd been driving. He'd screamed her name to try to warn her, but it had all happened so fast.

She'd been killed instantly.

What if he'd been driving? Could he have moved them out of the way in time? Or would he have died instead of her?

Sometimes, he wished that.

Why had God protected him, but not Eliza? He knew he wasn't supposed to wonder that, but he couldn't help it.

"What's wrong?" Snow asked quietly. "I'm sorry if I upset you."

"It's not your fault," Dominic said, not able to look up at her as he busied himself with shuffling the cards and setting them up for the next round. "I know God has a plan and loves us all, and we are not supposed to question why terrible things happen to good people. That is something I will never understand."

CHAPTER SIX

A few days later, now that she could finally stand and walk without passing out, Adriana stood in front of the house, staring out at the fields and the animals that were grazing. All she could see for miles were fields of snow and other Amish homes ranging in color from maroon to gray or white.

Adriana pulled the borrowed black winter coat even more tightly around her, thankful the Amish here used buttons and zippers, unlike some more traditional communities. Damaris and Constance had been lending her clothing, which made Adriana feel guilty, but she wouldn't be here much longer.

What a strange place this was. She'd been driving, not knowing where she was going, and somehow ended up in an Amish community. In a house of seven children, no less. Though she'd been smiling as she met them all, she'd wondered if they could see beyond her façade.

She was lying to them every moment of every day, yet they still took care of her. Adriana walked as quickly as she could to the phone shanty, which was much slower than she wanted to.

Though she wished she was with Megan more than anything, Adriana had to admit, this place was growing on her. The people were growing on her. She grabbed fistfuls of her deep purple skirt and apron as she walked, smiling at how comfortable she felt in Amish clothing, even Damaris' black boots she wore that were a bit too small.

Constance had offered to make her or buy her some *Englisher* clothing, but Adriana had asked for a few Amish dresses instead.

"Are you sure? Don't you want some jeans and sweaters from the store? I think you might be more comfortable wearing what you usually wear," Constance had offered.

"Actually, I think I might like Amish dresses better. I do want to fit in here, but it's not just that. I admire your way of life here, and I want to be a part of it. I know wearing the clothing won't make me Amish, but it might be symbolic of how much I appreciate you all helping me here. I'm not sure if that makes any sense," Adriana had said, furrowing her brow and shaking her head, suddenly feeling foolish.

Yes, she wanted to fit in. She wanted to fit in just in case Henry came looking for her. Maybe, just maybe, her new disguise would fool him.

And Adriana had let Constance believe it was just because she admired the Amish way of life. And Adriana did, of course. But that was not her main reason for wearing the Amish clothing.

"I understand, dear," Constance said, patting her hand. "Leave it to me."

Constance had sewn her some beautiful Amish dresses, and it was like Adriana had worn them her entire life.

Somehow, the dresses helped her feel at home, even though she'd never really feel at home without Megan. As each day passed, her recovery was more pronounced, and she knew whether they thought her memory was restored or not that she would be leaving this place soon, for Megan's sake.

It truly was a bittersweet feeling. Yes, she wanted to be with Megan again, but she'd miss this place.

Finally reaching the phone shanty, she fought to catch her breath as she opened the door and stepped inside to the tiny shed-like structure. She collapsed onto the stool and dialed Mrs. Clement's cell phone number from memory.

"Please, God, let Megan be safe," Adriana prayed.

"Hello?" the housekeeper said when she answered the phone.

"It's me, Adriana."

"Oh!" Mrs. Clement cried out, sobbing in relief. "Are you okay? Where are you?"

Adriana explained what had happened with the car crash and how Dominic's family was helping her.

"Oh, I'm so sorry this is all happening, dear." The other woman sniffed and blew her nose loudly.

"How is Megan? Is she hurt?"

"She's safe. Henry doesn't bother her much. He's been ignoring her, really. I've been keeping her company. She's so devastated and lonely. We had Jordan's funeral. I wish you could have been there."

"Me, too," Adriana said, a lump forming in her throat. "I wish more than anything I could have been there for Megan. She must be so hurt and confused."

"Henry told her that you're dead," Mrs. Clement said.

"I think we should keep it that way. If we tell her I'm alive, I'm afraid Henry will ask her questions, and she might slip up and tell him. You know how manipulative he is," Adriana said.

"You're right." Mrs. Clement started sniffling again. "Where are you?"

"It's probably best I don't tell you that, either. But I'm with a nice family, and they're taking care of me."

"Oh, good. I'm so glad you called. I also wanted to tell you Henry is having me spring clean the entire house and sort through Jordan's belongings, so that will give me an excuse to search the house thoroughly for the will and evidence."

"Well, that's great! Maybe it's hidden in her things. I'm so sorry, Mrs. Clement, but I better go. I sneaked out to make this call, and they might get worried. Thank you for taking care of Megan."

"Please call me as often as you can."

"I'll try."

Adriana hung up, then hurried back up the lane. She'd missed her own sister's funeral. Tears blurred Adriana's vision as she walked, and she quickly wiped them away.

"Oh, Jordan. I'm so sorry for all of this," Adriana whispered, wishing she could talk to her sister just one more time, even just to apologize.

When she finally reached the field again, she stopped, gasping for breath.

She sighed as she heard approaching footsteps. Expecting it to be Dominic, she said, "It's like I've stepped into a Laura Ingalls Wilder book."

"What's that?" a female voice asked, and Adriana swiveled around.

Her eyes widened when she saw that it was Damaris. She swallowed. The young woman had been very cold to her all this time, and Adriana had no idea why she disliked her so much. Honestly, Adriana was glad that she had healed up enough to care for herself. She didn't like depending on others to take care of her and bring her meals.

"She's a wonderful author who wrote a book about a house on the prairie. I think I read her books a long time ago," Adriana told her as Damaris was looking back at her thoughtfully. "Is there something wrong?"

Damaris tilted her head to the side. "Why would anybody hurt you?"

Adriana couldn't tell if she was genuinely asking or being snarky.

Adriana smiled ruefully and said, "Sometimes, Damaris, people want to hurt you to get something they want. You don't have to do something wrong to be hated."

She knew that more than anyone. Jordan had known that more than anyone.

"I came out here because I need to talk to you about something. I see the way my brother looks at you, and you have to know something. You see, if Dominic falls for you and if he wants to be with you, he would be shunned. He has officially joined the Amish church, so the rules are stricter for him. I know you're new here, so you don't know our rules, but if an Amish person is romantically involved with an *Englisher,* they could be shunned. An *Englisher* is anyone not Amish. And when a person is shunned, we are not allowed to eat at the same table as them and most do not speak to them."

"Oh, I had no idea." She'd feel terrible if that happened to Dominic because of her. "I don't want him to get in trouble."

Before Damaris could reply, Adriana started off into the fields.

"Where are you going?" Damaris called after her.

"For a walk," she replied. "I need to clear my head. I'll be fine."

Damaris groaned and hurried inside.

Adriana stood at the edge of the forest, staring at the crash site where her car had been, which must have been towed away at some point. As she stared, tears rolled down her cheeks.

Was that how she really would have ended up?

When Jordan had married Henry, Adriana had felt as though he was not the right man for her, that he didn't truly love her. She had no idea back then what Henry was truly capable of.

Over the years, Adriana had asked Jordan over and over if Henry was abusing her or hurting her in any way. It wasn't just the feeling Adriana had about Henry anymore, the feeling she'd had that he was dangerous ever since she'd met him. It wasn't just the way Adriana overheard him talking down to Jordan, criticizing everything from the way she walked to how she laughed.

When Jordan started getting bruises on her arms and face, blaming it on walking into a door or tripping over something, Adriana knew for sure. But Jordan continued to assure Adriana that she had a happy marriage, even defending Henry, saying he had never hurt her and never would.

Of course, Adriana knew that wasn't true. Henry must have threatened Jordan so she wouldn't tell.

Adriana tried to get Jordan to help her prove Henry was abusive by hiding cameras in the house, but Jordan had refused, even getting angry at Adriana. Adriana still didn't know why Jordan and Megan hadn't left Henry. Maybe Henry had threatened her, or maybe he'd brainwashed her.

Still, Adriana could have tried harder. How could she have let this happen to her sister?

Henry had killed Jordan.

He'd tried twice to kill Adriana.

What could stop him? Adriana wished more than anything that she could go to Jordan's house and search for something, anything that would prove Henry had killed her. But she couldn't until the new will was found.

"Oh, Megan," Adriana cried, wrapping her arms around herself, which did nothing to ward off the bitter wind. "I'm so sorry I'm not there with you."

She started moving toward the site of the crash, tears still streaming down her face, when large hands gently caught her and pulled her into a tender embrace.

She didn't have to look up to know it was Dominic. Adriana sobbed into his chest as he held her, saying, "It will be okay."

After a moment, she wiped her eyes and shook her head, suddenly embarrassed at her outward show of emotion. "I'm sorry. I'm fine. Really."

"You don't have to apologize for showing how you feel. You didn't do anything to deserve this. I'm sure of it."

"How can you be so sure?" she asked, her green eyes still wet with tears.

Dominic smiled at her as they walked and said, "You are a genuine person. I can sense it, even from the short time you've been here. You're kind and sincere. There's no way you did something to deserve that."

With each word he spoke, guilt stabbed at Adriana's heart. She hadn't done anything to deserve Henry trying to kill her, but after all the lies she'd told Dominic, she didn't deserve his trust.

Or whatever feelings he had for her. When he found out about all of her lies, would he ever want to speak to her again?

"How do you know I'm a genuine person?"

"I was a police officer with the Covert Police Detectives Unit during my time away from here. If anything, the job taught me how to read people. And I can tell you have a kind, pure heart," he told her, taking her hand.

"You were a cop?" Adriana asked, astounded. "But...you're Amish."

"I left for a while, then came back."

So many thoughts swirled in Adriana's brain. He thought she had a pure heart, yet she had been lying to him since they'd met.

Most importantly, he had been a police officer. Could he help her?

Should she tell him the truth?

"You were talking about Megan again. Who is she?" Dominic asked.

Adriana's stomach lurched. He'd heard her? "I don't know what you mean."

"You said you were sorry for not being there with Megan when I walked up to you. Do you remember who she is?"

"Um…" Adriana searched for words. How could she lie her way out of this one?

"Maybe you just remember the name and that you love her, but don't remember who she is yet," Dominic offered.

She sighed in relief, nodding. "Yes, that's it, I think."

Dominic patted her arm. "Don't worry, Snow. You'll remember in time."

In her head, she kept on trying to find the right words to tell him everything, but fear stopped her from voicing the truth.

Was he willing to be shunned for her when he didn't know her at all?

Thoughts tumbled tumultuously in her head, and before she knew it, they had arrived back at the house. Constance hurried out and led her inside.

"You had us so worried. Damaris said you told her that you were going for a walk. You shouldn't go out alone yet, not until you're fully healed."

"I am sorry for upsetting you." She looked from brother to mother, filled with guilt. "You're right. I'm sorry. I went back to the site of the crash, and I didn't even think about how it might worry you. I just wanted to get out of the house for a bit. I needed to clear my head."

Dominic stood there watching her; he was so engrossed in doing it that he had no idea his mother was watching him.

"Don't worry, Snow. I understand. You must be so confused right now. We're just glad you're here. I'm going to get dinner started," Constance said.

"Please, let me help," Adriana said, but she knew that cooking and doing the dishes wouldn't make up for the worry she'd caused Constance.

"No, no, dear. You're just barely able to walk. You should rest," Constance said.

"I insist. Please let me help. I feel well enough," Adriana said, not taking no for an answer as she walked into the kitchen.

***

As Damaris watched her brother and the strange woman, she looked at her mother in shock. "I haven't seen him laugh like that in years," Damaris said quiet enough so only her mother could hear.

After eating and cleaning up, they had all retired to the living room, where the younger children played board games or read books, as they usually did. The house was always filled with joyful noises between the children playing and talking with each other and the younger ones running around, but lately, Dominic had finally joined in on the fun again.

While Constance quilted and Damaris read a book, Dominic and Snow were engrossed in a conversation, laughing and joking as they played a game with the children on the floor. Daisy must have said something funny, because all of them smiled at her and erupted with hearty laughter. She had always been the clown in the family.

Constance smiled at Damaris and turned back to look at them. "I love seeing him so happy. My prayers have been answered, my child. The light has returned to his eyes."

"No! *Maam*, she's not Amish!" Damaris whispered.

"You think I don't know that?" Her mother smiled ruefully.

"Mother, you say that now because the woman has no recollection of her past. What if she finally remembers and wants to leave?"

"Then she will." Constance shrugged and continued her quilting.

Damaris tried reasoning with her. "And what if he leaves with her? If Dominic leaves this time, there is no coming back."

"But he will be happy, won't he? Damaris, look at your brother. That light in his eyes, that smile on his lips, that playfulness—Snow brought it all back. Now, if she does not want to become Amish and your brother chooses to follow her, do you honestly think I will do anything to stop him when his happiness is what I have prayed for?" Constance sighed happily, watching her son. "Yes, it would be terribly hard to see him leave again, and I do wish he would stay here forever. But I am praying that the Lord gives me peace about whatever he decides. I just want him to be happy again."

"I don't know why he cannot like Margaret. If he liked her, then he'd marry her and live here, close to us."

"What is wrong with Snow? She is caring and hardworking. Even tonight, she helped us cook and wash all the dishes, even though she probably didn't feel up to it. And she makes your brother happy. That's what matters. And who knows? What if she decided to join the Amish?"

"I doubt it. She probably has a family and a life she will want to go back to if she regains her memories. Besides, it's rare for outsiders to join."

"Anything could happen." Constance gave her another knowing smile and went back to her quilting. "Again, we need to support him with whatever he chooses. The Lord will help us."

But Damaris was not satisfied. She was having none of it. She wanted more than anything for her brother to be with Margaret, so Dominic could stay with them forever.

Damaris stormed out of the house, slamming the door behind her a bit harder than she'd meant to.

What was her brother thinking, keeping an *Englisher* here? And a beautiful one at that. Her long dark hair and beguiling green eyes would capture the attention of any young man.

This was not good. Not good at all. If he left again, Damaris knew it would shatter her mother's heart, even though she did say she just wanted him to be happy. It would devastate their younger siblings.

And Damaris would be heartbroken again.

For years, Damaris had been trying to get her brother to notice her best friend Margaret romantically. And now, after she had been so close, this woman—this *outsider*—was going to shatter it all.

Damaris walked into the dark barn and patted Apple's nose. While Dominic had been gone, gallivanting around with his *Englisher* wife, Damaris had taken care of Apple, and they'd bonded. She'd let herself believe Apple was *her* horse.

Then Dominic had come home, like nothing had ever happened, and Apple was his again. Just like with the farm, and his place in the family, it was like nothing had happened once Dominic returned.

Margaret would have been Damaris' ticket to having her brother stay here with them forever. She'd lost him once before, when he'd left the Amish to marry his *Englisher* wife. And it had ended tragically. Then, when their father had died, Dominic had left his job with the police force to come home and help *Maam* with the farm. He'd finally seen how he'd been wrong to leave them, asked for forgiveness, and was baptized into the church.

But Dominic was flighty. Just because he'd officially joined the Amish church didn't mean another pretty young woman couldn't convince him to leave again.

And she'd lose her only older brother. Again.

Damaris remembered the day Dominic had come back home after his wife had died. It was not what she'd expected at all.

"Dominic!" Damaris had cried, running out of the house when the hired driver had pulled into the driveway. Filled with excitement, she and her younger siblings bolted out of the house to greet him.

"You're home!" she shouted, jumping to throw her hands around his neck. He patted her on the back but didn't share her enthusiasm.

He didn't even bend down to pick her up and twirl her around, like he often did. He just stood there, saying hello somberly to her and their siblings. When *Maam* came outside last, Dominic's eyes filled with tears at the sight of her.

"*Maam*," he said, his voice cracking with bottled up emotions. He lifted his arms.

"My son!" *Maam* cried, running into his arms. Dominic immediately broke down into shaking sobs while their mother patted his back. "I'm so sorry about what happened to your *Fraa*."

"It happened so fast," Dominic said as Damaris watched the exchange. "We were driving in our car, and a truck ran a red-light and hit us. She was killed instantly, but somehow I survived."

Because Dominic hadn't called much or written to them while he'd been gone, they were just now finding out the details of how his wife had died.

"Why did I survive, *Maam*? Sometimes I wish..." Dominic began, then his words were overcome by sobs.

Damaris ran to him, hugging him around the waist. "Don't even think that, Dominic. We love you, and we want you here. God spared you so you could come home to us again." This was a blessing in disguise. Why couldn't her brother see that?

Dominic looked at her, then broke down in tears again. But finally, he hugged her back.

"I loved her, Damaris," he finally choked out.

Damaris knew there was so much more behind that one sentence, but he didn't need to speak the words. She understood everything else he wasn't saying.

"Thank you, Damaris, for saying that. And for taking care of Apple. You're such a good sister," Dominic croaked. He patted her head like she was a child.

She wasn't a child anymore. Couldn't he see that? While he'd been gone, especially after their father had died, who had taken care of *Maam* when she'd cried out in the night from losing the love of her life? Who had taken care of their five younger siblings when *Maam* had been crying in bed all day? Who had done the chores late at night and in the early morning before dawn?

Damaris had. Damaris had been there for *Maam* when Dominic hadn't.

She was a woman now, but she still needed her brother, especially now that *Daed* was gone.

Filled with so many emotions ranging from guilt to jealousy to relief, she had watched as Dominic and *Maam* walked into the house, arm in arm.

Leaving her behind, standing in the dusty driveway.

Damaris shook her head as Apple's whinnying brought her back to the present. He prodded her arm with his nose as if to rouse her from her memories.

"Apple, what are we going to do? We can't lose Dominic again. Now that *Daed* is gone... He's supposed to be the man of the house. *Maam* needs him. We need him." Damaris leaned forward, touching her nose to Apple's.

"I need him," she whispered, a lone tear stranded on her cheek.

***

As Dominic worked on the furniture he was building, his eyes searched around for Snow. She had said she would bring his lunch to him.

He wasn't hungry—he just missed her. He set down the tool in his hands and looked around. His workshop was a bit of a walk from the house, so he hoped that she had not gotten lost trying to find it.

Dominic smiled to himself as he turned back to his work. He felt happy, happier than he had been in a long time, and he knew it was all because of Snow. She brought light back into his life, and he believed that she was part of the Lord's plan for him.

69

"Dominic!"

At the sound of that voice, he resisted groaning outwardly. He knew that voice all too well. Margaret had no plans of leaving him alone anytime soon.

He straightened up and turned to look at her. "Hello, Margaret. How are you?"

"I am very well, Dominic." She smiled at him as she played with the frayed edges of her apron, her fiery red hair peeking out from underneath her head covering.

"Are you off to somewhere?" he asked, hoping that her answer would be yes.

"Oh, yes." She nodded eagerly. "I have some errands I have to run. I just saw you as I walked by, and I had to talk to you."

"How kind of you. Well, don't let me keep you. You should go on." He waved his hand, but she was rooted to the spot.

"So, I was wondering when you were going to come see my parents," she persisted, leaning toward him.

Dominic quirked a brow. What was she talking about?

"Why would I come see your parents?" He hadn't meant to blurt out the words in such a careless way, but his irritation was starting to get to him.

"Well, I thought it was obvious." Red tinted her cheeks.

Dominic groaned and ran a hand down his face. "Let me make *this* obvious. Margaret, I just don't feel that way about you, but one day you will meet someone who does. You just have to open your heart and seek the Lord's face. I don't want to court you. Not now, not ever."

70

She took a step back, arms crossed, a pained look on her face, as though she'd been punched in the stomach. "Look, maybe we just need to get to know each other better," she protested defiantly.

"No, Margaret," Dominic said with conviction. "It's not that. We've known each other our whole lives. I'm sorry. It's just not going to happen. In fact, I'm interested in someone else."

"What?" Margaret's entire face turned red now, and Dominic could envision smoke spurting from her ears. "Who is it? What's her name?"

As Dominic searched for the right words, they heard soft singing. Dominic looked to see who was approaching, and his face lit up. Snow was approaching, wearing a blue dress and a white apron that *Maam* had made for her. Her eyes were bright and smiling, and he walked down to meet her halfway.

"Sorry I took so long," she said. "I got a bit lost."

"That's okay. You're here, and that's what matters," Dominic said, grinning.

Margaret cleared her throat.

"Margaret, this is Snow. Snow, Margaret is Damaris' best friend."

"Hello. It's nice meeting you." Snow flashed a smile.

Margaret looked at her from head to toe condescendingly. "Likewise. Well, I should be going now."

As Margaret left, Snow and Dominic walked down the lane.

***

Adriana had to admit she was glad to see Margaret leave. Something about that woman made Adriana uneasy.

Yes, she had wanted to visit Dominic while he was at work, but the real reason she'd offered to bring him his lunch today was so she could make another secret phone call to Mrs. Clement before visiting Dominic at work. To her relief, Megan was still safe, though deep in mourning for her aunt and mother. Still, however, Mrs. Clement had not found the will or any hidden evidence at the estate.

Adriana hated keeping the fact that she was alive from Megan, but she and Mrs. Clement agreed it was the best option for both Megan's and Adriana's safety.

In her heart, Adriana knew she had to tell Dominic her story and ask him for help. And soon.

As Dominic and Adriana walked down the lane, ice covered the skeletal tree branches like a crystal glaze, sparkling in the sunlight, as a few lone flurries blew from the rooftops. Dominic smiled as he looked around at the view and nodded to Adriana. "Isn't it beautiful here?"

"Oh, yes," Adriana said. "I love it here. I think this must be the most beautiful place in the world."

And that wasn't a lie.

"I would definitely agree with that," Dominic said proudly.

"So, is it just me or did I just notice some animosity back there?" Adriana asked.

"Yes, you're not wrong. Margaret has had it in her head for a while that I am going to court her."

"Really? And are you?"

Dominic shrugged. "I have never loved her or liked her in that way. She knows it but keeps hoping. Actually, she considers you a threat."

Adriana stopped. "Really? Why?"

Dominic stopped and took Adriana's hand. "What can I say? You are not a threat to her because I don't love her. You are the one who has my heart. I need to be honest." He took a deep breath. They were such good friends, he hoped he wasn't about to ruin what they had, but he couldn't keep this from her any longer. "I'm not good with words. I know we are friends, and I hope this doesn't make you uncomfortable. I understand if you don't feel the same way, but I have to tell you this. I know you might have a family out there, but we have no way of knowing. All I know is I'm here with you now, Snow, and I love you."

With every word he spoke, Adriana's heart pounded faster and joy filled her soul. "I feel the same way, too, Dominic. It started as being grateful towards you for all you did, but it has grown into something else. You have a place in my heart. I love you, too." Her eyes wandered to the ground, as realization set in.

This was it. She couldn't lie to him anymore. It was time he knew the truth. All of it.

Dominic raised her hand to his lips and kissed her knuckles. "But?"

"Well, first of all, Damaris told me you'd be shunned if you left again."

"Of course, she did. I don't care about that. I'd do anything to be with you."

Adriana shook her head. "But there is so much I have to tell you. You don't know me, not really." Dread filled Adriana's belly. Would he reject her once she told him the truth? Never speak to her again? "Besides, I don't want you to be shunned." Just the thought of him being shunned for leaving with her made her feel guilty.

"Of course, I know you, Snow." Dominic reached up and gently touched her face.

Though she wanted to lean into him, she just looked into his eyes. "My name isn't Snow. It's Adriana Daniels."

"What? You remembered?" Dominic grinned. "That's great!"

"No." Adriana shook her head. What a mess she'd created. "I'm so sorry, Dominic. This entire time, I've been lying to you, but it was to protect all of us. I didn't have amnesia. I was afraid to tell you who I was."

Dominic stared at her, and she couldn't read his expression. Anger? Confusion? Hurt? All three?

"When you found me, I mentioned someone trying to kill me. My brother-in-law tried to kill me. Twice. Before the car crash, he sent an assassin to cut out my heart."

"This man sent someone to cut out your heart? What kind of sick person would do that?" Dominic asked, dumbfounded. "Who could do this to you?"

"It's a long story. Let me back up," Adriana said. "I have a child that needs me."

Dominic's eyes widened. "You have a child?"

"No, she's not my daughter." Adriana breathed in and said, "She's my niece, my sister's child, Megan."

Dominic slowly nodded. "Megan. That's the name you were saying in your sleep. And who is Jordan?"

"Jordan was my sister."

"Was? What happened to her?"

Adriana told him everything, starting from when Jordan had married Henry. She told Dominic how she'd suspected Henry was abusive, but Jordan had denied it for years, defending Henry. She told him about everything from Jordan's death to how she ended up here.

"She left me everything, including Megan, and he will stop at nothing to kill me so he can take it all. He doesn't even love her. He's keeping her from me just to hurt me," Adriana explained, then paused, trying again to read his expression. "I'm so sorry I lied. I didn't know what to do. I was afraid to tell you who I was, and I was afraid to make up fake information about myself, not sure if I could keep the story straight. So I just pretended to have amnesia. When you told me that you used to be a police officer, I wondered if you could help me somehow. I hope I haven't lost your trust and that you don't hate me. But if you do, I understand." Adriana looked at the snow-covered ground, expecting the worst.

She felt a tender hand upon her cheek, and she looked up to meet Dominic's kind eyes. "I told you I love you, and nothing could ever change that. I'm not mad at you, Snow. I mean, Adriana. Can I keep calling you Snow? I do like that name."

Adriana smiled. "Sure."

"I know my family won't be mad at you either. I understand why you lied. And I do want to help you. Yes, I used to be a police officer, and I can help you. Let me help you. Let's prove Henry is guilty…together. Also, you probably shouldn't tell anyone here the truth about who you are until after Henry is arrested, for your own safety. Don't worry. Everyone will understand."

"I hate lying to them. I've felt so guilty this whole time," she said.

And I can't believe how blessed I am to have found someone to help me and that he isn't mad at me for lying, Adriana thought.

"I know. But if you tell the entire church who you really are, word might get out. And if Henry is as powerful as you say, it could lead him right here. Why don't we go after him now and start our search for evidence?" Dominic asked.

"If Jordan left any evidence against him, it would probably be in her journals. She's always kept journals, ever since we were kids. I know a few places she might have them hidden that Henry doesn't know about. But to find them, we'd have to go to the house. I think he has security cameras, even ones Mrs. Clement doesn't know about. He would know I'm alive and try to kill me again. I'm all Megan has left. No." She shook her head. "I've been in contact with Mrs. Clement, and for now, Megan is safe. She's been searching the property. We have to wait until the new will is found. Then I will tell the police how he tried to kill me."

"Okay, I see what you mean. Well, for now, we can see a lawyer in town about the fake will. I know him from when I worked on the police force."

"Yes, let's do that. Wait, Dominic. There's something else. I'll have to leave after this is over. Damaris told me if you leave again, you'll be shunned. I think we both know this—us—can't happen without someone getting hurt."

Dominic smiled. "I loved and I lost a long time ago, Snow. I am not going to let that happen again. The good Lord who brought us together did not make a mistake. I will not let you go. If I have to leave the Amish and my family to be with you, I will."

"I couldn't ask you to do that," Adriana murmured. "It's too much of a sacrifice."

"You don't have to ask. It would be worth it to be with you, Snow. It's a choice I'm willing to make." Dominic wrapped his arms around her, and his nearness warmed her heart.

***

"Dominic, it's good to see you." The lawyer smiled at them as he welcomed them into his office. He was a young man in his late twenties and clapped Dominic on the back in a friendly way. "I haven't seen you since you worked for the Covert Police Detectives Unit."

"It's been a while. Thank you so much for seeing us on such short notice," Dominic said. "Adriana, this is Alec Becker, attorney-at-law."

"Just call me Alec. Nice to meet you, Adriana." He shook her hand firmly. "Please, have a seat." He gestured to two comfortable-looking leather chairs.

Adriana told Alec the entire situation. "How can we challenge the old, fake will?"

"Unless you can find the new one, there's not much we can do. You could contest the will for your niece, Megan's, share even if you can't find the newer will. You could do this by proving she signed the old one under duress and may have died intestate without a will. But it sounds like Henry's lawyer will rebut that," Alec told her. "But if you do find a new will, then the earlier one would be revoked, and presumably you would inherit. Or, if you could prove he murdered Jordan in order to inherit from her, the estate will pass as if he had predeceased her. But if the police and coroner believe her death was an accident, I am not sure how you will find any evidence to the contrary."

Adriana put a hand to her head as her mind swam, trying to grasp what Alec was saying. It was all so confusing. "I don't care about the money for me. I just want custody of Megan because it is not safe for her to be living with Henry. And I want her to inherit it all when she's older."

"Well, you could sue for custody, but that would alert Henry to the fact you are alive. Have you gone to the police about the car crash?"

"The car was burned, and it's been towed away. Besides, I don't think they'd be able to tell who exactly tampered with her brakes. All they would find out, if it wasn't burned too much, is someone cut her brakes. It's not like they left a signature," Dominic said.

"Well, I'm sorry. I wish I had better news. But until you find the current will, there is not much we can do," Alec said, his hands open on his desk. "I'm sorry."

Adriana barely heard what was said as Dominic thanked Alec and said goodbye. As they walked out of the office, Adriana hung her head, a storm of thoughts and questions raging in her mind. What would they do now? What *could* they do?

"I know that isn't what you wanted to hear," Dominic said, putting an arm around her shoulder. "We will have to find some other way."

"I don't know what else to do," Adriana said. "I just wish I could go search the estate myself."

"Maybe God is trying to teach you patience," Dominic said with a shrug.

"But Megan is in that house with that monster," Adriana said. "Just knowing that makes me feel so helpless. I just wish I could go to her."

"We will get her away from him, Adriana," Dominic said, taking Adriana into his arms. "I promise."

CHAPTER SEVEN

On Sunday afternoon, after church, the congregation gathered downstairs for their regular potluck lunch.

As the men mingled with the men and the women mingled with the women, Dominic was on the other side of the room, and Adriana felt as though he was an ocean away.

The service had been two-and-a-half hours long, mostly in Pennsylvania Dutch, a form of German. Thankfully, Constance was sitting next to her and translated as much as she could, but Adriana had only gleaned bits and pieces.

Feeling completely out of place at the potluck, she didn't know what to do or say. She wished she had something to do or help with. Relief filled her when Constance came to her rescue.

"Darling, let me introduce you to my friends," she said, looping her arm in Adriana's as they walked up to a group of chatting women who were speaking Pennsylvania Dutch, but then switched to English.

"Debbie, Marsha, Roberta, this is Snow, as we like to call her," Constance explained.

"Oh, we've heard so much about you," Debbie said. "All good things. Although, we are so sorry to hear about your car accident and how you lost your memory."

Adriana faked a smile, feeling like a terrible person for lying to these people.

"It's tragic. I can't even imagine surviving something like that," Roberta added, slowly shaking her head. "You poor dear."

"Well, you're staying with one of the sweetest ladies in all of Unity," Marsha said, beaming at Constance. "I hope she's taking good care of you."

"Constance and her family have been so kind to me, taking me in when they didn't even know me. I could never thank you enough." Adriana patted Constance's arm, which was resting on her own.

They took me in, and they trust me, even though I've been lying to them, Adriana thought. *Will they really not be angry with me after this is over?*

"Well, I see the way Dominic looks at you," Marsha said, smiling ruefully. "Is there anything going on with the two of you?"

"Uh…" Feeling as though she was treading water and slipping under the waves, Adriana fought for breath. "We are friends. He did rescue me, but I am very grateful to the entire family."

"I see." Debbie clicked her tongue, and the three women gave each other mischievous looks.

"As she said, ladies, they are just friends. Nothing is going on there. Well, we need to get the food ready, Snow. Will you help me?" Constance said, and before Adriana could answer, Constance turned her away from the woman and led her to the door.

"Nice to meet you!" Adriana called over her shoulder. What was going on with Constance?

Did she know something? Had Dominic told her?

"Sorry to pull you away like that," Constance said once they were out of ear shot. "I got nervous. I don't want them getting the wrong idea."

"Nervous? Why?" Adriana asked.

"I do want my son to be happy, especially after all he's been through," Constance explained. "Did you know he'd be shunned if he left?"

"Yes, I know. I don't want him to get in trouble. Did you know he told me he loves me?"

"Yes, I did, and I was happy to hear it," Constance said. Adriana expected worry to be in Constance's eyes, but her eyes were filled with hope. "You make my son happier than he has been in years, Snow. I see how he looks at you. To be honest, I would be happy to see you together, no matter where you choose to live. I do hope you'd consider joining the Amish, but I understand that's unlikely. I don't want to lose him again, but it is his choice. I just want you to know what could happen if things go wrong."

"I understand. Thank you for telling me."

"Also... You wouldn't lead him on, right?" Constance asked, wringing her hands.

"No, of course not. I love Dominic," Adriana said in a rush, feeling uneasy. Did Constance really think she'd lead Dominic on?

"I'm sorry. I don't want to seem too forward," Constance said, then smiled. "Of course, you wouldn't do that. You have brought joy into our home again, Snow, and I am grateful for that. Now, let's go get the food ready."

Constance took Adriana's arm again, and they made their way to the food table, where Adriana helped Constance set out a large sandwich platter with meats, cheeses, bread, and toppings.

"I must have left the mustard in the buggy," Constance said. "I'll be right back."

As Adriana continued to work, she looked up when she heard whispering.

"You know, someone is trying to kill that woman. Why is she here?"

"You're right. She's putting us all in danger. She shouldn't be here."

"What if the amnesia is all an act? Maybe she really does remember and she is lying to everyone."

With each word she heard, Adriana's heart plunged deeper into depths of dread. Did they know the truth about her?

Unable to listen to another word, she hurried through the crowd of people and bolted out the door, feeling as though she was suffocating.

Were people seeing right through her lies? What if they figured out who was after her and led Henry right to her?

Maybe it was time to leave.

As she watched the dancing tree branches in the air, she heard approaching footsteps, and she turned around.

"Snow?" an elderly Amish man with a kind smile asked as he approached. "I heard you were doing better. I'm glad to see you up and walking around. Praise the Lord you survived that crash. I'm Sid Hoffman. I was in the buggy ahead of you when your car crashed. I helped Dominic look for you, but he is the one who found you."

She wanted to tell him how she remembered what had happened right before the crash, how she'd been trying to avoid hitting his buggy and the other car. Instead, she said, "Oh, yes. I don't remember, but I am glad you were not hurt. Thank you for helping Dominic look for me."

"Well, I am just glad to see you well. Have a nice day." He put on his hat and ambled toward his buggy.

What a nice man. Adriana smiled, glad he hadn't been hurt.

Someone else walked toward her. It was the young woman Dominic had introduced to her as Margaret.

Adriana tried to put on a happy face. "Hello," she said, but Margaret gave her a once over again and crossed her arms.

"I am just here to tell you something for your own good," Margaret spat out. "It would never work out between you and Dominic. You're not Amish. You should stay away from him so you don't end up hurting him, if you care about him at all. He wouldn't leave his family and community for you. He could never love you enough to leave."

"Yesterday he told me he loves me and would leave to be with me if he had to, even if he was shunned. Constance just told me she would be happy to see us together."

Margaret kept staring at Adriana, but Adriana didn't miss the suppressed look of surprise on her face. "You would be selfish enough to take him away from his family if you have to leave here? You know this has happened to him before, right?"

Adriana squinted in confusion. "What?"

"Oh, you don't know? Dominic didn't tell you?"

No, he didn't, Adriana thought in dismay.

"I guess he doesn't know you well enough to tell you about it, yet. Anyway, when that didn't work out, it destroyed him, and he came back. He joined the church and vowed to never leave the Amish again. You want to make him break his vows and crush his mother and siblings?" Margaret took a step closer with every sentence she spoke, and as Adriana's confidence weakened, she found herself taking defensive steps backwards. Margaret's biting words cut into Adriana, breaking her resolve.

Maybe he doesn't know me well enough yet to tell me about his past, she thought. *Maybe she's right.*

Adriana shook her head, trying to calm the storm of questions raging in her mind. Why hadn't Dominic told her about this when he'd professed his love to her?

Right now, she couldn't worry about that. She'd ask Dominic about it later.

As Adriana's mind wandered even farther, she noticed Margaret staring at her with a sickening glare.

Adriana spun around to walk toward the frosted fields. She already had enough stress and did not need a jealous woman thrown into the mix. Margaret huffed and stalked off.

"Hello, there!" It was Dominic's sing-song voice this time. He caught up to Adriana and took her hand in his. "Are you okay? I saw you walk out. What were you talking to Margaret about?"

"I'm fine." Adriana looked away from his searching eyes. She didn't exactly want to tell him about how the other women had been talking about her.

"Something is bothering you. I can tell," he pressed. "What did she say to you?"

Adriana sighed, figuring she might as well be honest with him. They walked behind the church building so no one would overhear. "I heard some of the women talking about me inside, saying how I should leave because someone is trying to kill me, and it's dangerous for me to be here. They think my amnesia is an act. I think they're figuring it out. Do you think they know what's going on? Should I leave?" The words tumbled out faster and faster as her panic grew. She also explained what Margaret had said to her.

"It's okay," Dominic said, pulling her into a hug. "It's just gossip. And Margaret means well, but she doesn't know what's best for us. Right now, the best place for you is right here."

CHAPTER EIGHT

The sun radiated through the blinds, making Adriana squint. Was it morning already?

Adriana rubbed her eyes, giving up on sleep. There was so much on her mind, she'd tossed and turned all night, then had finally fallen asleep about an hour ago. Yesterday, she'd called Mrs. Clement, only to find out that the housekeeper had still not found the new will or evidence. Henry was ignoring Megan for the most part.

After quietly getting up and getting dressed, Adriana went out to the barn to talk to the animals. That always made her feel better.

Her decision made, she turned around to see Damaris a few steps away from her.

"Why are you out here so early?" Damaris asked.

"Couldn't sleep."

"Can I talk to you?"

"Sure. About what?" Adriana asked quietly.

"My brother."

"Damaris, I..." she started saying, but Damaris interrupted her.

"Just listen. I have to say something. You should leave him now because all you are going to do is break his heart and he will have nowhere to go to."

"What are you talking about? I would never break Dominic's heart. I love him. And what do you mean by him having nowhere to go to?"

87

Damaris sighed and looked at her. "About six years ago, when he was nineteen, during Rumspringa, Dominic left the community before he got baptized into the church. He fell in love, and he did not return. A year later, he got married to Eliza. He got a job in law enforcement. He was happy; they were happy. Two years later, they were in a terrible car crash. Eliza died, but Dominic survived. Did he ever tell you any of this?"

Adriana gasped, and her hand flew to her mouth. Why hadn't he told her this?

"No. Margaret said yesterday that something had happened, but I didn't get the chance to ask him yet. I figured he'd tell me when he was ready.' Adriana's brow furrowed. It wasn't really Damaris' place to be telling her all about Dominic's past like this. "Don't you think he should be the one to tell me all of this?"

Damaris held up her hands. "Snow, I'm only trying to help. He doesn' like to talk about it, so who knows how long it would take for him to finally tell you? It's time you know."

Adriana crossed her arms but let Damaris continue.

"My brother was devastated, and he returned a broken man, a youn widower. The community accepted him back. He was ready to be a part o the church, and he was baptized into it, committing to remain Amish fc life. I admit that ever since then, my brother has been going about his day without feeling. I doubted that he would ever be happy again. But he foun you, and he is happy again."

"Isn't that a good thing?" Adriana asked, filled with confusion. Wa this why Damaris was telling her about all this?

From the look on Damaris' face, that couldn't be it. As Adriana took in Damaris' intense and accusing expression, dread settled in her stomach.

Adriana hated confrontation. At the thought of it, at the thought of her being in the wrong, she began to tremble.

Damaris continued, "Maybe right now, but not long-term. You come with uncertainty—lots of it. Right now, you think you love him, but who's to say when the truth is revealed about your past, you won't hurt him? Who's to say you won't leave him as well? He will follow you and leave the community, but when you realize that you don't love him or that you're already married, you will break up with him. Because he's been baptized into the church, he'd be shunned for leaving, and he might not want to come back again. He might not get another chance, Snow. Let my brother go. If you care about him, leave us."

Adriana shook her head as tears rolled down her face. "I love your brother and that will never change. My heart belongs to Dominic." She whipped around and hurried towards the house, leaving Damaris behind. She burst through the kitchen door to see Constance chopping vegetables for a stew. Wiping her tears, Adriana collapsed at the kitchen table, her body shaking with sobs.

Why had Dominic's sister said such things to her? What had she ever done to her?

"My dear, what is wrong?" Constance asked, dropping everything to sit beside Adriana.

Adriana told her everything that had just happened with Damaris.

"You can't leave, Snow. You know he loves you," Constance told Snow. "You are making my son happier than I've seen him in years. If you leave, I fear he may go back to the man he was before."

"And I love him, too, but maybe Damaris is right. I think me leaving is what is best for him," she said as she wiped tears from her eyes.

"How can this be best for him? How can you leaving be best for the both of you?"

"The world outside is very dangerous for me. Those people who hurt me are still out there, and they are not going to stop until I am dead. I do not want him to deal with my problems." When she saw the questioning look on Constance's face, Snow added, "Especially, if something happens to me."

"But you can fight the odds together," Constance insisted. "And maybe you could live here together. With us."

Adriana smiled and hugged Constance tightly. "Thank you for taking a complete stranger in and accepting me into your heart and your life. I will forever be grateful." As she was about to step out the door, she stopped and turned. "There is something you should know. My name is Adriana. I should go. Again, thank you."

She walked out the door before Constance could protest or stop her.

When she was almost at the woods, she heard her name being called.

"Adriana!" Dominic ran toward her.

"How did you—" Adriana stopped, turning to face him.

"My mother told me you're leaving. We agreed to do this together Snow."

90

"Your family would be devastated if you left here to be with me. I can't do that to you or them. I have to do what's best for Megan, and that might mean living with her at my sister's estate. I have to put her first. And why didn't you tell me about Eliza?" Hurt filled her again at the thought of how he hadn't felt comfortable enough with her to share that part of him.

"Damaris told you, didn't she?" He didn't wait for Adriana's reply but shook his head, taking a deep breath. "I didn't tell you because I thought it might make you tell me you don't want to be with me so I don't make the same mistake twice. I thought that maybe if you knew what had happened, you'd tell me you didn't want to be with me in order to protect me, so I wouldn't leave my family again and get shunned. But this is my choice to make, Snow. I mean…Adriana. Sorry. I'll have to get used to that." Dominic smiled a bit, then turned serious. "If you and Megan want to live at the estate, then you should. I am ready to leave here again to be with you. I would rather take a chance on our love than stay here for the rest of my life wondering what could have been, going back to the empty man I was. You've awakened my frozen heart, Snow. It's like I've been sleepwalking all these years, but your love woke me up from the spell I was under."

Adriana smiled, looking up into his eyes. "You woke me up, too."

"Now, let's go together," Dominic said as he held her hands tighter.

"Dominic, this is not your fight." She started protesting, but he kissed her.

When he let her go, he smiled and said, "Where you go, I go. Your fight is my fight. After you get custody of Megan, we can create a family here with her," Dominic said to Adriana. "If that's what you and Megan want."

"It's what I want, but I'll have to ask Megan." She had never been more sure of anything in her life. This place opened up new wonders to her every day and felt more like home to her than anywhere else ever had.

"Are you sure you want to live here? What about the estate?"

"More than sure. If it's okay with Megan, I'll sell it. It's full of terrible memories anyway. She might want a fresh start. But if she wants to live there, then I will do that."

"You do whatever you think is best for Megan. And whatever you decide, I will stay by your side." Dominic held her close.

"I have to call Mrs. Clement at the phone shanty. Henry is probably at work, but I want to make sure." Adriana dialed the housekeeper's cell phone number, and she answered on the first ring.

"Adriana? How are you?"

"I'm okay. I'm with Dominic, and I told him everything. He wants to help me find evidence against Henry. He used to be a police officer so he could really help us out."

"Good. We need his help now more than ever. Henry is sending Megan to boarding school in Europe, and he's having her make the trip alone. He could easily afford to fly with her or send someone to escort her there, but he's having her go alone. I heard him on the phone telling someone that anything could happen to a young girl traveling alone. I think he's planning on staging an accident for her," Mrs. Clement said, her words rushing together as she spoke quickly.

Adriana's heart sank to the floor. "I can't let that happen. Not again. I didn't stop him from killing my sister, but I will stop him from killing my niece. I know I said I'd wait until you found the will, but I can't any longer. We need to come right now. Is Henry home?"

"He's still at work. You might have a few hours if you come now. He said he was working late tonight."

"We will be there soon." Adriana hung up, filled with hope for the first time in a long time. "Okay, let's go," Adriana said to Dominic with determination.

After speaking with Dominic's family and hiring a driver, Adriana and Dominic left the community, and the hired driver took them to Jordan's mansion.

As Adriana sat in the back seat of the car, her foot bounced and she wrung her hands with anxiety. Was Megan safe? She must have felt so alone all this time.

With Adriana out of the picture now, she knew Henry would do whatever needed to be done to keep the inheritance. Adriana was saddened for all that had happened to them, her sister's death, and her own close call with death. All because of Henry's greediness.

"It is going to be okay. Evil won't prevail," Dominic said comfortingly, resting his hand on hers to calm her. She stopped fidgeting as calmness and warmth flooded through her.

"Thank you," Adriana said with a grateful smile. She would always be grateful to him and his family for the help they had rendered her. Without knowing who she was, they had cared for her. Otherwise, she would be dead by now, leaving Megan with that horrible man.

When they arrived, Adriana bolted from the car and ran toward the house. Mrs. Clement opened the door immediately, as though she'd been waiting by the door for them to arrive. The stout housekeeper dashed through the door toward Adriana with surprising speed and pulled her into a hug.

"I am so glad to see you alive and well," Mrs. Clement said, squeezing Adriana even tighter.

Dominic got out of the car, paid the driver, and walked toward them.

"You must be Dominic," Mrs. Clement said, smiling at him, finally releasing Adriana.

"Yes, this is Dominic. Dominic, this is Mrs. Clement," Adriana said.

"Thank you so much for taking care of Adriana," Mrs. Clement said.

"It was our pleasure. If it wasn't for the car wreck, we probably would have never met," Dominic realized out loud.

"So how is Megan? Where is she?" Adriana asked.

"I tried my best to look after her, like I promised. Henry has been civil to her, mostly ignoring her. She must be upstairs in her room doing her school work," Mrs. Clement said. "She faked being sick today and stayed home from school. She's been doing that lately. As you asked, I didn't tell her you're alive."

"Well, I'm here now, and I'll be searching the house and the property, so she will figure it out anyway. I'll go talk to her."

Adriana hurried up the stairs, her heart racing. She went down the hallway, to Megan's door. It was locked. She pounded on the door. "Megan! Megan!" she called.

"Adriana?" Megan cried from the other side of the door. "Adriana, is that you?" Megan tumbled out into the hallway, flinging her arms around her aunt. "Angel! You're alive!"

"Oh, Megan," Adriana said. "I am so sorry. I'll explain everything and why I was gone for so long." Tears poured from Adriana's eyes as she hugged her niece.

"Henry told me you were dead like my mom, that I would never get to see you again!" Megan cried.

"No, I'm not dead, as you can see," Adriana said.

"Where have you been? I was so scared. Henry said he is sending me off to boarding school. He kept saying you were dead, but I was hoping you were still alive, hiding somewhere." Megan held Adriana even tighter.

While filled with tenderness for her niece, Adriana's fingers curled into a fist as indignation against Henry filled her. Henry was indeed a horrible person. She wished her sister had not married him, but Jordan had been too trusting. It had been too late when she realized how cruel he was.

"I'm here now, and nothing is going to happen to you," Adriana said. "I won't let him send you away to boarding school. Henry tried to kill me, but I survived. Dominic and his family saved my life."

"Who's Dominic?" Megan asked, looking at Dominic. "Him?"

Adriana smiled. "Yes. Megan, this is Dominic, and he's my special friend. He helped me to come save you and put Henry in jail," Adriana said.

"I like you, then," Megan said with a grin, then hugged Dominic.

"I like you too, Megan. I can tell we're going to be great friends," Dominic said, giving Adriana a smile.

Adriana was filled with joy at the sight of her favorite people in the world meeting for the first time. She mouthed a "thank you" to Dominic. With his help, Henry would be put away for a very long time.

"So," Adriana said, "what do you say we look for some evidence? Jordan always kept a journal, ever since we were kids. I think maybe she hid them where Henry would never know to look."

"Great idea," Megan said. "Let's start in her favorite place: the garden."

For the next several hours, the four of them searched the garden, looking for anything Jordan might have left behind: journals, photos, videos, anything. They dug holes all over the yard.

"I don't think it's here," Adriana said. "Maybe we should move on to somewhere else."

"I think you're right. I thought it would be here, though. Mom spent most of her free time out here with me. This was what we did together," Megan said, a wistful look on her face as she leaned on her propped-up shovel.

"What about the piano?" Mrs. Clement suggested. "She played that with you, Megan."

"Good idea," Dominic said. "Maybe it's inside, where Henry wouldn't think to look."

Hopeful, the four of them dashed into the house. They opened the baby grand piano, looking inside it and inside the piano bench, even underneath it.

Where else could it be?

Adriana felt so dejected that she'd barely noticed Megan's eyes filling with tears. The girl turned and ran, hurrying up the stairs.

"I'll go talk to her," Adriana said to Mrs. Clement and Dominic, then went up the stairs after her niece.

Adriana slowly opened Megan's bedroom door to see the girl sitting on the bed, crying.

"Megan, I'm so sorry. We didn't mean to upset you. I'm sorry we haven't found anything yet," Adriana said.

"I thought Mom would have left something behind for us to prove Henry hurt her. Why haven't we found it yet? What if she forgot to hide it for us? What if we never find it?" Megan said between sobs, her small shoulders shaking. Adriana had never seen her niece cry this hard, and she pulled her into her arms, her heart breaking for the child.

Megan's trembling hand clung to the pendant around her neck.

"Did your mom give you that necklace, Megan?"

Megan sniffed, wiped her eyes, and nodded. "I never take it off. It's special."

"It's beautiful. May I see it?"

Megan nodded and held out the locket to Adriana as far as the chain allowed. Adriana tried to open it. "Is it a locket?"

"No, it doesn't open," Megan said. "I've tried so many times."

It seemed a bit odd, since the necklace was definitely big enough to be a locket. Adriana flipped it over, studying the inscription on the back that was written in tiny letters, barely legible.

Your heart holds the answers. Your angel holds the key.

Adriana read inscription over and over. "Megan, this is a clue. A riddle."

"Really?" Megan's eyes lit up. "Dominic! Mrs. Clement!" she called.

Dominic and Mrs. Clement ran up the stairs, breathless.

"What's wrong?" Mrs. Clement asked.

"Did you find something?" Dominic asked.

"There is a clue on the necklace Mom gave me!" Megan cried, jumping off the bed.

"Since you were a toddler, you called me Angel because you couldn't pronounce Adriana," Adriana said, tenderness filling her heart with the fond memories of Megan toddling around.

"And your necklace!" Megan cried out so loudly Adriana jumped, pointing to the necklace around Adriana's neck. "Mom gave you a necklace too. A key. She gave you a key, and she gave me a locket."

Adriana felt for the tiny gold key that she'd never removed from her neck ever since her sister had given her the precious gift a few months ago. "Do you see a small keyhole on your necklace?"

They each quickly removed their necklaces.

"It's small, but it's there. I always wondered why there was a hole in it," Megan said.

"Here, Megan. You can do the honors." Adriana put the key in her niece's hand.

98

Megan took the tiny key in her trembling fingers, placing it into the tiny opening on the side of the locket. She turned it once, and the locket snapped open.

"Oh, my goodness!" Megan murmured. "It worked."

"Jordan," Adriana whispered, looking up at the ceiling. "Thank you."

"What's inside?" Dominic asked, coming closer, curiosity clearly taking him over.

"It's a tiny chip," Megan said, carefully removing a small rectangle from the locket. "What is it?"

"Probably images or video files," Dominic said. "We have to keep that safe."

"It's so tiny," Mrs. Clement breathed. "I've never seen anything like it."

The loud sound of a door slamming downstairs made them all tense.

"Is he home early?" Adriana asked.

"Quick! Put it back," Dominic said, and Megan quickly put the chip back in the locket and on her neck. Adriana fumbled to put her key necklace back on, since she always wore it, and there was a chance Henry would notice it not on her neck.

"You got it?" Adriana whispered to Megan.

The girl nodded.

Adriana eyed Mrs. Clement fiddling with her phone. "What are you doing?" she whispered.

Before anyone could answer, Henry was already walking down the hallway, and as his quick footsteps resounded on the floor, Adriana's heart pounded harder with each step.

"Adriana!" his voice boomed as he appeared in the doorway. "I told you not to come back. Who are you?" he demanded, staring at Dominic.

"The guy who will kick your butt if you hurt anyone here," Dominic said with a glower and a growl, walking toward him. Much taller than Henry, Dominic towered over him, but Henry's eyes didn't waver and he didn't step back.

Finally, Henry set his eyes on Adriana. "What are you doing here?"

"I told you I'd find the evidence I need to prove you killed Jordan. And we've found it," Adriana said, her voice full of confidence as she crossed her arms.

And this time, she didn't have to fake it.

"What on earth are you talking about? You're delusional," Henry spat out, but Adriana didn't miss the flicker of nervousness in his eyes.

He was scared. For the first time, Adriana saw fear in Henry's eyes.

"You can't prove anything," he stammered.

"We know you married Jordan for her money. You knew I inherited everything and had custody of Megan, so you tried to hide Jordan's current will, and you tried to have me killed. First, with a hired assassin, then cutting my brakes. But I survived, and I'm coming for you. We have photos and video files that Jordan left for us. So go ahead, keep saying we can't prove anything." Adriana said, slowly walking toward him as she spoke. The last part was a bluff. She hadn't seen what was on the chip yet, but she was confident Jordan had left either photos or video files on it incriminating Henry. "Also, Dominic here was a police officer for the Covert Police Detectives Unit and still has connections."

"I'd be happy to make a citizen's arrest right here," Dominic said coolly, cracking his knuckles.

Henry backed out of the doorway slowly. "No. It was all for nothing," he muttered.

"What was for nothing, Henry?" Megan demanded, her voice surprisingly powerful for coming from such a small frame. "How you hurt her or pushed her down the stairs? You are a bully!"

Megan's words resounded through the house, and she radiated truth and determination.

And somehow, though she was only thirteen years old, she made the grown man who had killed her mother cower in fear before her.

"I was supposed to inherit everything," Henry said, holding his hands up and backing away. "This wasn't supposed to happen."

"You're going to jail!" Megan screamed at him.

Henry turned and bolted.

Dominic was after him in a flash, tackling him in the hallway. Adriana was right on their heels, grabbing his feet while Dominic secured Henry's hands behind his back.

"Someone get a rope or something to tie him up!" Dominic called. "And call the cops!"

Megan came forward with a bathrobe tie.

"That'll work," Dominic said with a chuckle.

"You have nothing on me! I'll have you all arrested for breaking and entering!" Henry shouted, kicking and fighting.

"Oh, I already called the cops," Mrs. Clement said, holding up her phone. "I did it when he got here, because I figured something might happen. And I have been recording this since he got here."

"Ah, so that's what you were doing," Adriana said with a nod. "Nice."

"They're here," Megan said as sirens sounded in the distance.

CHAPTER NINE

After they'd turned over the evidence chip to the police that contained video files of Henry's abuse and the will, which even contained medical reports of Jordan's injuries, Adriana was informed that Henry had reported that she was missing a few weeks back.

"Of course, he would do such a thing so he wouldn't be as suspicious," Adriana said, shaking her head at how manipulative Henry could be.

It had taken hours for the detective and his team to look through the videos. Adriana refused to watch any of them; it would only make her sad seeing what Henry had done to her sister.

The entire time, Dominic had stayed by Adriana and Megan's sides.

"According to the evidence, we suspect Henry married Jordan to secure a seat on the board of the software company, and so that he could inherit the entire company and everything else after her death. That gave him a motive to kill her. Henry paid his lawyer, Nathan Brown, to use the older version of the will, which stated everything was left to Henry," the police officer explained to Adriana. "Jordan did make the new will with a different lawyer, George Houser, who Henry somehow tracked down and also bribed to keep quiet. As you know, Henry has many connections, and he used them to find Mr. Houser. That is why Mr. Houser told you the new will didn't exist. These lawyers violated the lawyer's code of ethical conduct. They will be charged and disbarred. Even if they do testify against Henry, they will never practice law again."

Adriana squeezed Dominic's hand. She'd known Henry was smart and manipulative, but hearing the police officer explain it made it all the more real.

The police officer continued, "Even though he hired the assassin to kill you, whom we hope to track down soon, cutting your brakes was a backup plan. Also, we found a secret camera in the house that your sister must have had installed, which recorded when he pushed her down the stairs. He killed Jordan. We have more than enough on him for murder, solicitation of murder, and attempted murder, and bribing two lawyers to commit fraud. He'll be going away for a long time."

***

"Thank you for doing that with me," Adriana said to Dominic for what seemed to be the hundredth time after Henry had been arrested. Their hired driver was driving the three of them back to Unity after they answered questions from the police at the station. For now, they would go home, but they would have to return later on for the trial.

Dominic took her hand. "I love you, and I will always stand by your side."

Adriana wasn't concerned about the inheritance for herself—she never had been. She wanted Megan to have it. All Adriana wanted was for Henry to pay for what he had done to them and to be locked away so he couldn't hurt anyone else again.

She was grateful that she had Dominic in her life. He and Megan gave her the strength she needed to get through this.

"We did it," Dominic said. "Now we can finally move on."

"God did it," Adriana said with a smile. God had given them the strength to go through the trial. He had given her the comfort of Dominic and his family who always supported her. "Wait. Before we go to Unity, I think we should visit Jordan's grave. I did miss the funeral while I was recovering in Unity, so I'd like to pay my respects."

"Of course," Dominic said.

"That's a great idea," Megan added.

They gave directions to the driver, and when they arrived at the cemetery, they quietly got out of the car.

Just the sight of Jordan's tombstone brought tears to Adriana's eyes and formed a lump in her throat. "I wish you could have met her, Dominic. She was a wonderful mother and sister." Adriana put an arm around Megan's shoulders.

"She was," Megan agreed. "The best mom ever."

They approached the grave, and tears streamed down Adriana's face. "Jordan, you were the best sister I could have ever hoped for. I'm so sorry things happened the way they did, and I know you had your reasons for not leaving Henry. Maybe he threatened you or told you he'd hurt Megan. I know you were probably protecting Megan, doing what you thought was best. I'm just sorry I didn't convince you to get away from him before he…" Adriana put her hands over her face, which did nothing to cover the sounds of her sobs as her heart wrenched. "I wish I could have saved your life, that could have prevented this from happening," she said through her tears, feeling Dominic's and Megan's arms around her. "I want you to know I'm going to take care of Megan. She's going to have a loving home, and I'll always be there for her as her guardian. We are beginning a brand-new life. And when she is older, the inheritance will be hers."

Megan patted Adriana's back. "I know I'm safe with you, Aunt Adriana." The girl turned to her mother's tombstone. "It's going to be okay, Mom. I know Angel will take care of me. We'll be a family together."

Adriana nodded, smiling through her tears. "Always, Megan."

Tears were still wet on their cheeks as they finally got back in the car. For the next several minutes, no one spoke as they drove, but then Megan began to talk about the Amish community, asking question after question. Happy that the mood was lightening, Adriana contently listened as Dominic told Megan all about the Amish lifestyle and his family.

"We're almost there, Megan. Are you excited?" Adriana asked as they approached Unity.

"Yes! I can't wait to meet everyone. I can't believe you have so younger brothers and sisters. I'll have fun all the time!" Megan said, bouncing in her seat.

"That's for sure." Dominic laughed. "There is never a boring moment in our house with so many children."

The car drove down the lane, and Megan pressed her nose up against the glass, pointing out everything she saw.

"Here we are," Dominic said as the driver parked the car in the driveway. Megan opened the door and climbed out just as Constance and all the children hurried out of the house to greet them.

"Hello!" Megan cried.

"You must be Megan. We are so happy you are here. I'm Constance, and these are all my children. You met Dominic. Oldest to youngest, this is Damaris, Delphine, Danny, Dean, Daisy, David, and Desmond," Constance said, gesturing to each child.

Megan just looked at them all for a moment, as if processing all the new information. "I'm so happy to meet you all!" she cried, running to them and greeting each of them. Danny stiffened at first when Megan hugged him, but Adriana didn't miss how his serious expression softened into a smile.

"I'm so glad you're here!" Daisy cried, grabbing Megan's hands. "We are going to be the best of friends. I just know it. I can teach you how to ride horses and take care of the animals, and you can tell me all about what it's like to be an *Englisher*. We can play games outside and jump rope. Oh, and I will teach you how to play all kinds of games like Dutch Blitz."

"If you want to learn how to feed the animals, you have to wake up early," Desmond said, yawning. "I don't like waking up early."

"I don't mind," Megan said with a laugh. "I want to learn everything about this place."

"I'm allergic to the hay, so I don't like going in the barn," Dean said, then sneezed.

"You're allergic to everything, Dean!" Daisy said, and they all laughed.

As the other children talked with Megan, Delphine hid behind her mother's skirt, watching.

"Hello, there. Are you Delphine?" Megan asked, kneeling down to the small girl.

107

Delphine nodded, and after a moment, she walked up to Megan and hugged her.

"I think they are going to be the best of friends," Adriana said to Dominic with a smile.

"Come on, let's go play hide and seek!" Daisy yelled, and all the children ran to the backyard.

***

"Dominic," Damaris said, pulling her brother aside as the children went out back and Constance and Adriana went inside the house. "I need to talk to you about something."

"Can we do this later? So much is happening right now with Megan arriving, and I want to make sure she feels at home," Dominic said, starting to walk away.

"No. Wait!" Damaris said, much louder than she'd intended.

Dominic stopped and stared at her. "What is it? What's wrong?"

"Come on. Let's go in the barn." Pivoting on her heel, she stalked off toward the barn, not bothering to look behind her to see if he was following.

"What's going on? You're acting strange," Dominic said as they stepped inside. The scent of hay and manure filled the air.

"I need to apologize to you," Damaris began.

"Look, I know you and Adriana didn't get off on the right foot, but she'll forgive you for being rude to her." Dominic waved his hand. "It' okay, Damaris."

108

"Listen to me, brother!" Damaris shouted, and the horses looked up from their hay, ears pinned back as if listening in on their conversation. She took a deep breath, calming herself, and said in a softer tone, "For once, stop trying to fix everything, and just listen to what I have to say. No interrupting."

"Okay. I won't interrupt. I'm sorry." Dominic raised his hands, palms up. "Continue."

"I have to apologize for a lot more than just being rude to Adriana. You need to understand why I was. As you know, I wanted you to end up with Margaret, but I don't think you know the real reason why."

Dominic just looked at her silently, eyebrows raised.

"The truth is, I thought if you married Margaret, you'd stay here forever with us. I was worried you might fall for Adriana, then you'd leave again, like you did before. And you would have, if she'd asked you to."

"Yes, I told her I would do anything to be with her."

"Don't you see? I couldn't bear to lose you again, Dominic. When you left last time, it destroyed me. You've always been my true best friend, even more so than Margaret. And after *Daed* died, I realized you were the last father figure left in my life. I need you, brother. It was selfish of me, but I did some wrong things trying to keep you here," Damaris explained. "And not only was I sad when you were gone, but I was angry at you for leaving, too. You left me here, as the next oldest child, to do everything. I needed your help. But you were gone."

"Oh, Damaris, you've always been my best friend, too. But I didn't realize you felt that way. I'm sorry," Dominic said, grabbing her hand. "I guess I never realized all of this. I should have known you'd step up and take all the responsibility while I was gone. I was ignorant. I should have known."

Finally, he understood her perspective. She felt relief and some satisfaction, but it was squandered by dread filling her belly.

"There's something else. While you were gone, I prayed for you to return. I didn't care what price you had to pay, I just wanted you back here for my own selfish reasons. But today I was thinking about the day you came back, and how sad you were that Eliza had died. I was just happy you were back, and I didn't realize it then, but I realize it now... I think my prayers caused Eliza to die." Tears rolled down her cheeks. "Please, don't hate me."

"Damaris!" Dominic gently grasped her shoulders. "I could never hate you. I'll love you no matter what. But why do you think your prayers caused her to die?"

"Because I prayed for you to come back, and I didn't care how or why. I think God killed Eliza to answer my prayers." Damaris let out a sob, and her shoulders shook as Dominic hugged her.

"No, Damaris. That's not true. I don't know why Eliza died, but it's not your fault. It was the drunk driver's fault. Please don't think for a second that you are guilty."

She sniffed, reaching up to wipe her eyes as he released her. "You sure?"

"I'm sure. It's not your fault at all. Don't feel bad about asking God to bring me back here. God works in mysterious ways, and often we don't know the reasons why."

"Well… There is more I have to tell you," she squeaked out.

Would he hate her after hearing what she was about to confess?

He gave her a confused look, as if wondering what else she possibly had to admit.

"I was so intent on keeping you here and separating you and Adriana that I was the one who spread the rumors about her at church," Damaris admitted, staring down at the hay-covered barn floor. "Somehow, I thought it might make Adriana uncomfortable enough to leave, then I thought you might forget about her and finally court Margaret. It was a terrible, stupid idea. I see now how wrong I was. I am so sorry, and I understand if I've lost your trust. Clearly, the two of you are meant to be together. I just hope you can forgive me one day for being such a vile, wretched sister."

Silence.

For several long moments, Damaris couldn't lift her eyes from the floor, just wondering what was going through her brother's mind. Would he ever speak to her again?

She'd been so focused on keeping her best friend and brother here, but did she just lose him forever in the process?

"Look at me, sister."

Wiping hot tears from her eyes, she slowly looked up at her brother, who was smiling down at her tenderly.

"You are the most loyal, dedicated, determined person I know, Damaris. And I am proud to call you my sister," Dominic said.

"What?" Damaris choked out, sobs wracking her shoulders. "You don't hate me? You're not mad at me?"

"No. I love Adriana. Nothing could have kept us apart. But that's beside the point. You went through great lengths to keep me here with you, and though it was unconventional, you have a good heart. Our family is meant to stick together. And I have you to thank for making me realize that. I love you, Damaris, and nothing will ever change that," Dominic said, pulling his sister into a tight hug.

"I love you, too," Damaris said, crying into his shoulder. She knew her tears and nose were staining his white shirt, but neither of them cared. "I'll apologize to Adriana, too. Truly, I hope we can be friends, but I doubt she will want to after how awful I've been to her."

"She will forgive you. Don't worry. You'll be best friends before you know it."

All that mattered was that they were together again, and this time Damaris knew her brother was here for good.

***

"So what are you going to do?" Constance asked that evening as they sat outside the house, watching Megan while she played with the other children. She fit in with them like she'd grown up there.

"I have to deal with the estate of my sister, Jordan. Now that Henry has no claim to the estate, I'm officially Megan's guardian. I have to do what I think is best for her. She has been through a lot," Adriana said. Her niece had so much strength and she was proud of her. First, she had lost her father at a young age, then her mother, and she had thought she had lost her aunt. Adriana wanted Megan not to be scared or worry about life. She wanted her to start afresh, and though she knew it was impossible, Adriana wished she could protect Megan from everything.

Adriana knew she needed to make a decision soon. There were already new murmurs in the Amish community about her and Dominic getting married.

"Do you like it here?" Adriana asked Megan the next day. They were out in the backyard having a snack on a blanket under the trees.

"Yes, I love it here! I want to stay here forever. It's so different from home. People here are nice. I like Constance, I like all Dominic's brothers and sisters, and I like Dominic," Megan said.

"Living here is different from out there," Adriana said.

"I know. There are no TVs here, but that's okay with me. I love books instead. I like living here, Angel, as long as it is with you and Uncle Dominic," Megan said.

"Are you sure?"

"I'm sure. I promise."

Adriana practically leapt across the blanket and hugged her niece. "I'm so glad to hear that, Megan," she said, filled with peace. And of course, if Megan wanted to leave when she was older, she was free to do so. "But what about your home? Do you want to go back there?"

"No," Megan said. She pulled away, shaking her head adamantly. "I never want to go back there. It's just filled with bad memories. So many

113

bad things happened there. Henry hurt my mom there, and he hurt me there. I'm sorry, but I don't want to go back."

"I completely understand, Megan, and you have nothing to be sorry for. Well, I have something to ask you, then. I was thinking about selling the house and business and putting the money in a bank account and some investments for you to have when you are older. What do you think about that? You wouldn't be able to go there again. It would belong to someone else. We'd live here instead. Would you be sad to leave your school and your friends?"

Megan furrowed her eyebrows, pondering Adriana's question. She grinned. "Really, I have friends at school, I guess, but I don't have any best friends. I don't fit in. Most of the girls are snobby and mean to me. I don't really like my school. I think moving here is a very good idea. I like the other kids here. I want to live here, and I don't want to go back to that house ever again. It just reminds me of Mom dying and how mean Henry was."

"Then this is our new home now." Adriana put her arm around her niece's shoulders. "Megan, welcome home."

***

"Are you sure you want to do this?" Dominic asked as they spoke in the barn.

Adriana patted Apple's nose. "Yes. Being in this community makes me happy and at peace. That's the life I want for Megan and me, and I want to join the church and become Amish," Adriana said. She had thought hard about her decision and she was confident in it.

"I am so glad to hear that," Dominic said, pulling her close. She could feel his heartbeat against his chest, and she smiled, closing her eyes.

He was the reason she had chosen to stay in the community. He had told her that wherever she decided to go, he would follow her. He had been willing to make the sacrifice of leaving his people to be with her and Megan, and she knew how much that meant to him. He would have been away from his family who loved him. She also knew his family was worried about him leaving and being shunned by the community. Seeing him radiate happiness now, she knew she had made the right decision.

"Now that you've decided, there is something I want to ask you," Dominic said, his eyes gleaming with joy.

Anticipation swirled through Adriana. Was he about to ask her what she'd been hoping for?

"The Amish don't wear rings, so I don't have a ring for you," he began.

She didn't care one bit about a ring. She just wanted him.

"You came into my life and woke me up from a sleep-like trance I didn't even know I was in. I was numb. Empty. I felt like I had no purpose. Then when you woke up, you woke me up. You made me alive again."

Adriana overflowed with love and gratitude, and she squeezed his hand tighter.

"I might have brought you out of that car wreckage, but you rescued me, Snow. To me, you will always be Snow. My dear Snow."

She grinned. "That's fine with me."

"I didn't save you. You saved me. And I love you with everything in me." Dominic's eyes shone with tears as he poured out his heart to her, and he pulled her close to him. "And I want to spend the rest of my life enjoying every second with you, exploring this whole new world of wonder that you've opened my eyes to. Snow, will you marry me?"

Adriana didn't hesitate, not even for one millisecond. "Yes!"

Dominic kissed her, and she wrapped her arms around him. Meeting him had changed her life. For the first time she felt truly happy and loved. She cared so much about him and was grateful that he was in her life. Her life was certainly not perfect, and she was still hurt from losing her sister, but God had given her an opportunity to be happy, and she was going to make the most of it.

Constance was excited when they told her about their decision to get married and build their home. With tears in her eyes, she hugged her daughter-in-law to be. "Thank you so much, Adriana. I have never seen him this happy. Now! We need to go about planning the wedding!"

"Why do I feel like she's going to go overboard?" Dominic mumbled. With simple Amish weddings, there were no decorations, cake, or flower to splurge on. However, Amish weddings were often quite large with enormous amounts of food, and Dominic knew his mother would probabl invite every person they'd ever met.

She had never had the opportunity to do so when he married Eliza, bu this time around, he was going to give her free rein.

And as for Mrs. Clement, now that the house was being sold, Adrian had given her a nice retirement package, and the housekeeper was going t travel to Europe, as she'd always wanted. But not before she would atten the wedding, of course.

"Does this mean you'll be my new dad? And Adriana, will you be my...mom?" Megan asked when they told her the news.

Adriana and Dominic looked at each other, unsure about how Megan felt about this.

"Well," Adriana said. "As you know, you're going to live with me. After Dominic and I get married, he will move in with us. Dominic will be your uncle and I'm still your aunt, of course. What do you think about that? Is that okay with you?"

"Okay? *Okay?*" Megan said, jumping up from her chair. "It's more than okay. It's the best thing ever!" She jumped up and down with excitement, and Adriana laughed out loud, filled with so much joy she thought she might burst. Adriana's heart swelled with love for her niece.

***

Dominic was working every day on their new home which was on a piece of land his father had given to him. He was building their home with the help of his brothers and friends, and they hoped it would be completed before their wedding, which would be that upcoming November.

Adriana had taken classes, was learning Pennsylvania Dutch, and had been baptized into the Amish church after the elders approved her. Finally, she was part of a family again. Megan was still too young to be baptized into the church and would have to make that decision when she was older.

"Adriana," Damaris said.

Adriana looked up from the dress she was stitching. In front of her were Damaris and Margaret.

She smiled at both women. "Good afternoon."

Damaris sat beside Adriana, taking her hands in hers. "I must apologize to you, Adriana. You were in need of comfort and help, and I was only mean to you. I'm not sure if you know this or not, but I was the one who spread the rumor about you that day at church. I already told everyone involved that I lied and those things I said about you were not true."

Adriana's first instinct was to jolt backward, away from Damaris. How could Damaris have done that to her, and humiliated her at church, when she needed friends most of all? What kind of person did something so cruel?

Adriana wanted to reply angrily, but when she looked into Damaris' eyes, she saw genuine repentance.

Damaris continued, "I just wanted my brother to be happy. I didn't want him to be hurt like before, and I was afraid you'd make him want to leave the Amish again. But I was wrong about the two of you. He's the happiest I have ever seen him. He loves you, and I know that you love him. Please forgive me. I would like us to be friends, Adriana." Damaris looked at the floor. "But I understand if you want nothing to do with me."

Adriana smiled. She held no grudges against Damaris. She understood that she had been trying to protect her brother from being hurt. "Damaris, now I see how loyal you are to your brother. I want to be your friend, too. All that is history. We're family now," Adriana said, giving Damaris a hug.

"I also have something to say," Margaret said, sitting on the other side of Adriana. "You were new here and didn't know anyone, and I should have been welcoming to you, lending you support with all you went through. I'm sorry for being horrible to you. This was out of insecurity. When you came into the picture, I was upset and scared. Please forgive me. You two clearly belong together."

Adriana hugged Margaret. "We all make mistakes, even if we have good intentions," Adriana said. "Of course, I forgive both of you. To be honest, I hope we can be good friends."

The three women sat down and got lost in conversation, discussing everything from the wedding food to the house where Adriana and Dominic would live. As she talked with them, Adriana could tell this truly was the start of a new friendship. She had never seen any of this coming—being married to a man she loved, with an amazing child, and such loving family and friends around her.

Dominic came into the house, but Adriana barely noticed, she was so lost in conversation with her friends.

"Well, this is a sight I thought I'd never see," Dominic muttered in confusion, twisting his hat in his hands.

The three women looked at him, looked at each other, and laughed.

Adriana felt right at home, knowing that she was loved. She hadn't been looking for love, but she had found it in so many forms, and she would be forever grateful.

*****

About the Author

Ashley Emma knew she wanted to be a novelist for as long as she can remember, and her first love was writing in the fantasy genre. She began writing books for fun at a young age, completing her first novel at age 12 and publishing it at age 16. She was home schooled and was blessed with the opportunity to spend her time focusing on reading and writing.

Ashley went on to write eight more manuscripts before age 25 when she also became a multi-bestselling author.

She now makes a full-time income with her self-published books, which is a dream come true.

She owns Fearless Publishing House where she helps other aspiring authors achieve their dreams of publishing their own books. Ashley lives in Maine with her husband and children. She plans on releasing several more books in the near future.

Visit her at ashleyemmaauthor.com or email her at amisbookwriter@gmail.com. She loves to hear from her readers!

If you enjoyed this book, would you consider leaving a review on Amazon? It greatly helps both the author and readers alike.

Leave your Amazon review here:

https://www.amazon.com/Amish-Alias-Romantic-Suspense-Detectives-ebook/dp/B07ZCJBWJL

Thank you!

GET 4 OF ASHLEY EMMA'S AMISH EBOOKS FOR FREE

www.AshleyEmmaAuthor.com

Download free Amish eBooks at www.AshleyEmmaAuthor.com, including the exclusive, secret prequel to Undercover Amish!

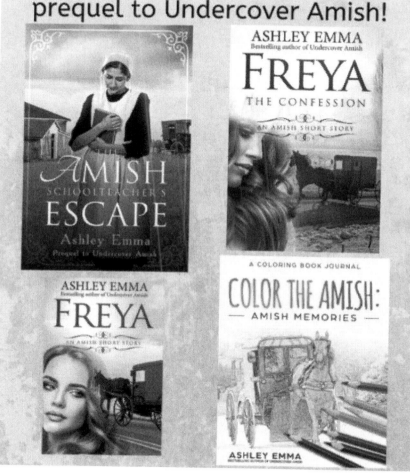

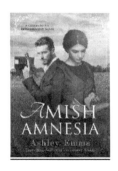

Coming soon:

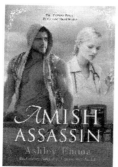  

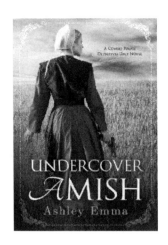

UNDERCOVER AMISH

(This series can be read out of order or as standalone novels.)

Detective Olivia Mast would rather run through gunfire than return to her former Amish community in Unity, Maine, where she killed her abusive husband in self-defense.

Olivia covertly investigates a murder there while protecting the man she dated as a teen: Isaac Troyer, a potential target.

When Olivia tells Isaac she is a detective, will he be willing to break Amish rules to help her arrest the killer?

Undercover Amish was a finalist in Maine Romance Writers Strut Your Stuff Competition 2015 where it received 26 out of 27 points and has 455+ Amazon reviews!

Buy here: https://www.amazon.com/Undercover-Amish-Covert-Police Detectives-ebook/dp/B01L6JE49G

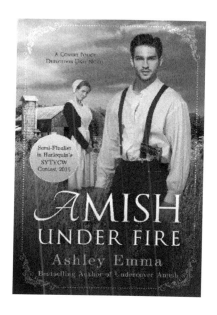

After Maria Mast's abusive ex-boyfriend is arrested for being involved in sex trafficking and modern-day slavery, she thinks that she and her son Carter can safely return to her Amish community.

But the danger has only just begun.

Someone begins stalking her, and they want blood and revenge.

Agent Derek Turner of Covert Police Detectives Unit is assigned as her bodyguard and goes with her to her Amish community in Unity, Maine.

Maria's secretive eyes, painful past, and cautious demeanor intrigue him.

As the human trafficking ring begins to target the Amish community, Derek wonders if the distraction of her will cost him his career...and Maria's life.

Click here to buy: http://a.co/fT6D7sM

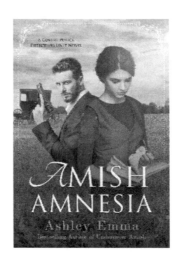

When Officer Jefferson Martin witnesses a young woman being hit by a car near his campsite, all thoughts of vacation vanish as the car speeds off.

When the malnourished, battered woman wakes up, she can't remember anything before the accident. They don't know her name, so they call her Jane.

When someone breaks into her hospital room and tries to kill her before getting away, Jefferson volunteers to protect Jane around the clock. He takes her back to their Kennebunkport beach house along with his upbeat sister Estella and his friend who served with him overseas in the Marine Corps, Ben Banks.

At first Jane's stalker leaves strange notes, but then his attacks become bolder and more dangerous.

Jane gradually remembers an Amish farm and wonders if that's where she's from...or if she was held captive there.

But the more Jefferson falls for her, the more persistent the stalker becomes in making Jane miserable...and in taking her life.

Buy here: https://www.amazon.com/gp/product/B07SDSFV3J

FREE EBOOK

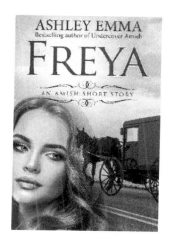

After Freya Wilson accidentally hits an Amish man with her car in a storm, will she have the courage to tell his family the truth—especially after she meets his handsome brother?

Get it free: https://www.amazon.com/Freya-Amish-Short-Ashley-Emma-ebook/dp/B01MSP03UX

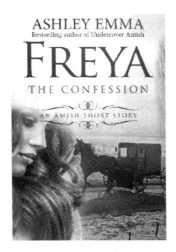

Adam Lapp expected the woman who killed his brother accidentally with her car to be heartless and cruel. He never expected her to a timid, kind, and beautiful woman who is running for her life from a controlling ex who wants her dead.

When Freya Wilson asks him to take her to his family so she can tell them the truth, he agrees.

Will she find hope in the ashes, or just more darkness and sorrow?

https://www.amazon.com/Freya-Confession-Amish-Short-Forgiveness-ebook/dp/B076PQF5FS

Ever wondered what it would be like to live in an Amish community? Now you can find out in this true story with photos.

https://www.amazon.com/Ashleys-Amish-Adventures-Outsider-community-ebook/dp/B01N5714WE

Excerpt from Amish Alias

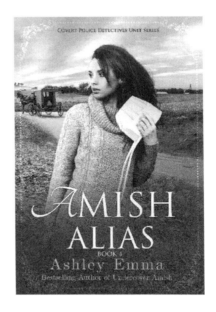

(This Series Can Be Read Out Of Order Or As Standalone Novels)

Chapter One

"Mom, are we there yet?" nine-year-old Charlotte Cooper asked from the back seat of her parents' van. Her legs pumped up and down in anticipation. Mom had said they were going to a farm where her aunt lived, and she couldn't wait to see the animals. The ride was taking forever.

"Just a few more minutes, honey," Mom said from the driver's seat.

Charlotte put her coloring book down and patted the lollipop in her pocket Mommy had given her for the trip. She was tempted to eat it now but decided to save it for the ride home. She hoped it wouldn't melt in her pocket. The van was hot even though she was wearing shorts and her favorite pink princess T-shirt. Charlotte shoved her damp blonde curls out of her eyes.

The van passed a yellow diamond-shaped sign that had a black silhouette of a horse and carriage on it. "Mommy, what does that sign mean?"

"It's a warning to drive slowly because there are horses and buggies on the road here."

"*What?* Horses and bugs?"

"No." Mom smiled. "They're called buggies. They're like the carriages you've seen in your storybooks. Except they are not pumpkin-shaped. They are black and shaped more like a box."

Charlotte imagined a black box being pulled by a horse. If she were a princess, she would like a pumpkin carriage much better. "Why are there buggies here?"

"The folks who live in this area don't drive cars."

They don't drive cars? Charlotte thought. "Then what do they drive?"

"They only drive buggies," Mom said.

How fast do buggies go? Charlotte wondered. *Not fast as a car, I bet.* "Why would anyone not drive a car? They're so much faster than buggies."

"I know, honey. Some people are just...different." Mom glanced

133

at Charlotte in the rear-view mirror. "But being different isn't a bad thing."

Charlotte gazed out the window. Even though they had just passed a pizza place a few minutes ago, all she could see now were huge fields and plain-looking houses.

There was nothing around. This looked like a boring place to live. What did people do to have fun here besides play outside?

A horse and carriage rumbled past them on the unpaved road going in the other direction. A girl wearing a blue dress and a white bonnet sat on the top seat, guiding a dark brown horse. She looked just like a picture Charlotte had seen in her history book at school. "Look, Mom." Charlotte pointed at the big black box on wheels.

"It's not polite to point, Charlie."

Charlotte dropped her hand to her side. "Why is that girl dressed like a pilgrim, Mom? She's wearing a bonnet. Are we near Plymouth Plantation?"

Mom didn't answer. Maybe she was too distracted. She seemed really focused on the mailbox up ahead.

"We're here," Mom said and turned onto a long driveway.

Charlotte gaped at the chocolate-colored horses in the fields and the clucking chickens congregating in the front yard. The van bounced over bumps on the gravel path leading to a huge tan house with bright blue curtains hanging in the windows. The dark red roof had a large metal pipe coming out of the top with smoke coming out of it, and behind the house stood a big red barn. Charlotte wondered how many animals were in there.

Mom parked the van and helped Charlotte out. "I'm going inside to talk to your Aunt Esther. I don't want to bring you inside because... Well... You should just wait here. I won't be long."

"Can I walk around?"

Before Mom could answer, a young boy about Charlotte's age walked out of the barn. He saw them and waved.

"Can I go play with him?" Charlotte asked.

"Hi!" The boy ran over. "I've never seen you around here before. Want to go see the animals in the barn?"

"Can I go in the barn with him?" Charlotte asked her mother.

"What's your name?" Mom asked the boy. "Is Esther your *Maam*?"

"I'm Elijah. No, she's not my mother. My *Maam* and *Daed* are out running errands, so I'm playing here until they get back. My parents are best friends with Esther and Irvin. I come here all the time. I know my way around the barn real well."

Mom crossed her arms and bit her lip, then looked at Charlotte. "I suppose you can go in. But stay away from the horses."

"We will, ma'am," said Elijah.

Charlotte and Elijah took off running toward the barn. They ran into the dim interior and she breathed in. It smelled like hay and animals, just like the county fair she had gone to last fall with her mom and dad. To the left, she heard pigs squealing. To the right, she heard sheep bleating.

Which animals should we go see first? Charlotte wondered, tapping her toes on the hay-covered floor.

135

Elijah leaned over the edge of the sheep pen, patting a lamb's nose. He was dressed in plain black and white clothing and a straw hat. His brown hair reached the collar of his white shirt. He even wore suspenders. Charlotte glanced down at her princess T-shirt and wondered why he didn't dress like other kids at her school. Every kid she knew wore cool T-shirts. *Why are the people here dressed in such plain, old-fashioned clothes?*

Charlotte stepped forward. He turned around, looked at her, and grinned. "So what's your name, anyway?"

"I'm Charlotte. Well, you can call me Charlie."

"Charlie? That's a boy's name."

"It's my nickname. I like it."

"Suit yourself. Where you from?"

"Biddeford, Maine. Where are you from?"

"I live in Smyrna, Maine."

"Oh." Charlotte raised an eyebrow. Smyrna? Where was that?

Elijah smiled. "It's a bigger Amish community in northern Maine."

Charlotte shrugged. "Never heard of it."

Elijah shrugged. "Want to pet the sheep?"

"Yeah." They climbed up onto some boards stacked along the edge of the enclosure. Several of the animals sniffed their fingers and let out high-pitched noises. "They sound like people," Charlotte said. "The lambs sound like babies crying, and the big sheep sound like adults making sheep noises."

They laughed at that, and when the biggest sheep looked at them and cried *baaa* loudly, they laughed even harder.

Charlotte looked at the boy next to her, who was still watching the sheep. A small smear of dirt covered some of the freckles on his cheek, and his brown eyes sparkled when he laughed. The hands that gripped the wooden boards of the sheep pen looked strong. She wondered what it would be like if he held her hand. As she watched Elijah tenderly stroke the nose of a sheep, she smiled.

When one lamb made an especially loud, funny noise that sounded like a baby crying, Elijah threw his head back as he laughed, and his hat fell off. Charlotte snatched it up and turned it over in her hands. "Wow. I've never held a straw hat before. We don't have these where I live. I thought people only wore ones like these in the olden days."

Elijah shrugged. "What's wrong with that?"

"Nothing." Charlotte smiled shyly and offered it back to him. "Here you go."

Elijah held up his hand. "You can keep it if you want." He smiled at her with those dark eyes.

Charlotte got a funny feeling in her stomach. It was the same way she felt just before saying her lines on stage in the school play. She knew she should say, "Thank you," like Mom had taught her. But she couldn't speak the words. Instead, she took the lollipop out of her pocket and handed it to him.

"Thanks," Elijah said, eyes wide.

"You're welcome."

Elijah gestured to Charlie's ankle. "Hey, what happened to your ankle?"

Charlie looked down at the familiar sight of the zig-zagging surgical scars that marred her ankle. "I've had a lot of surgeries on my ankle. When I was born it wasn't formed right, but now it's all better and I can run and jump like other kids."

"Does it hurt?"

"No, not anymore. But it hurt when I had the surgeries. I had, like, six surgeries."

"Wow, really?"

"Charlotte!" Mom called. "We have to leave. Right now."

"Thanks for the hat, Elijah." Charlotte turned to leave. Then she stopped, turned around, and kissed him on the cheek.

Embarrassment flushed Elijah's cheeks.

Uh oh. Her own face heated, Charlotte sprinted toward her mother's voice.

"Get in the car," Mom said. "Your aunt refused to speak with us. She wants us to leave."

Charlotte had never heard her mother sound so upset. She climbed into the van, and Mom hastily buckled her in.

"Why didn't she want to talk to us, Mom?" Charlotte said.

Mom sniffed and shook her head. "It's hard to explain, baby."

"Why are you crying, Mom?"

"I just wanted to talk to my sister. And she wanted us to go away."

"That's not very nice," Charlotte said.

"I know, Charlie. Some people aren't nice. Remember that."

The van sped down the driveway as Charlotte clutched the straw hat.

"Why are you going so fast?" Charlotte said and craned her neck, hoping to see Elijah. She saw him standing outside the barn with one hand holding the lollipop and the other hand on his cheek where she'd kissed him. He was smiling crookedly.

Mom looked in the rearview mirror at Charlotte.

"Sorry," Mom said and slowed down.

Charlotte settled in her seat. She hoped she'd see Elijah again, and maybe he'd be her very own prince charming like in her fairytale books.

But Mom never took her to the farm again.

Chapter Two

Fifteen years later

"Hi, Mom," twenty-four-year-old Charlie said, stepping into her mother's hospital room in the cancer ward. "I brought you Queen Anne's lace, your favorite." She set the vase of white flowers on her mom's bedside table.

"Oh, thank you, honey." Mom smiled, but her face looked thin and pale, a bright scarf covering her head. "Come sit with me." She patted the edge of the bed, and Charlie sat down, taking her mother's frail hand.

"You know why Queen Anne's lace are my favorite flowers?" Mom asked quietly.

Charlie shook her head.

"Growing up in the Amish community, we'd get tons of Queen Anne's lace in the fields every summer. My sister, Esther, and I would try to pick as much as we could before the grass was cut down for hay. At the end of every August, we'd also check all around for milkweed and look for monarch caterpillars before they were destroyed. We'd try to save as many of them as we could. We'd put them in jars and watch them make their chrysalises, then watch in amazement as they transformed into butterflies and escaped them. I used to promise myself that I'd get out into the world one day, just like the butterflies, and leave the Amish community behind. I knew it would be painful to leave everyone and everything I knew, but it would be worth it."

"And was it?" Charlie asked, leaning in close.

"Of course. It was both—painful and worth it. I don't regret leaving though. I never have. I miss my family, and I wish I could talk to them, but it was their choice to shun me. Not mine." Determination still shone in Mom's tired eyes. "I had already been baptized into the church when I left. That's why I was shunned. I still don't understand that rule. I still don't understand so many of their rules. I couldn't bear a life without music, and the Amish aren't allowed to play instruments. I wanted to go to college, but that's forbidden, too. Then there was your father, the Englisher, the outsider. It was too much for them, even for Esther. She swore she would never shun me. In the end, she turned her back on me, too."

Mom stared at the Queen Anne's lace, as if memories of her childhood were coming back to her. She wiped away a tear.

"And that's why she turned you away that day you took me to see her," Charlie concluded.

"Yes. Honestly, I've been so hurt, but I'm not angry with her. I don't want to hold a grudge. I can't decide if we should try to contact her or not to tell her I'm..." Mom's voice trailed off, and she blew out a lungful of air. She shook her head and looked down. "She wouldn't come to see me, anyway. There's no point."

"Really? Your own sister wouldn't come to see you, even under these circumstances?" Charlie gasped.

"I doubt it. She'd risk being shunned if she did." Mom patted Charlie's hand. "Don't get me wrong. I loved growing up Amish. There are so many wonderful things about it. They help each other in hard times, and they're the most tightly knit group of people I've ever met. Their faith is rock solid, most of the time. But most people only see their quaint, simple lifestyle and don't realize the Amish are human, too. They make mistakes just like the rest of us. Sometimes they gossip or say harsh things."

"Of course. Everyone does that," Charlie said.

Mom continued. "And they have such strict rules. Rules that were too confining for me. Once your father taught me how to play the piano at the old museum, I couldn't understand why they wouldn't allow such a beautiful instrument that can even be used to worship the Lord."

Mom shook her head. "I just had to leave. But I will always miss my family. I'll miss how God and family always came first, how it was their priority. Life was simpler, and people were close. We worked hard, but we had a lot of fun." Mom's face lit up. "We'd play so many games outside, and even all kinds of board games inside. Even work events were fun. And the food... Don't get me started on the delicious food. Pies, cakes, casseroles, homemade bread... I spent countless hours cooking and baking with my mother and sisters. There are many things I've missed. But I'm so glad I left because I married your father and had my two beautiful daughters. I wouldn't trade you two for anything. I wouldn't ever go back and do it differently."

Gratitude swelled in Charlie's chest, and she swallowed a lump in her throat. "But how could Aunt Esther do that to you? I just don't understand."

Mom shrugged her frail shoulders, and the hospital gown rustled with the movement. "She didn't want to end up like me—shunned. I don't blame her. It's not her fault, really. It's all their strict rules. I don't think God would want us to cut off friends and family when they do something wrong. And I didn't even do anything wrong by leaving. I'll never see it their way." Mom hiked her chin in defiance.

What had her mother been like at Charlie's age? Charlie smiled, imagining Mom as a determined, confident young woman. "Well, your community shouldn't have done that to you, Mom. Especially Aunt Esther, your own sister."

"I don't want that to paint you a negative picture of the Amish. They really are wonderful people, and it's beautiful there. You probably would have loved growing up there."

Charlie shook her head with so much emphasis that loose tendrils of hair fell from her ponytail. "No. I'm glad we live here. I wouldn't have liked those rules either. I'm glad you left, Mom. You made the right choice."

***

Elijah Hochstettler trudged into his small house after a long day of work in the community store with Irvin. He pulled off his boots, loosened his suspenders, and started washing his hands, getting ready to go to dinner at the Holts' house. He splashed water on his beardless face, the trademark of a single Amish man, thinking of his married friends who all had beards. Sometimes he felt like he was the last single man in the entire community.

He sat on his small bed with a sigh and looked around his tiny home. From this spot, he could see almost the entire structure. The community had built this house for him when he'd moved here when he was eighteen, just after his family had died. The Holts had been looking out for him ever since.

His dining room and living room were one room, and the bathroom was in the corner. It was a small cabin, but he was grateful that Irvin and the other men in the community had helped him build it. Someday he wanted to build a real house, if he ever found a woman to settle down with.

Another night alone. He wished he had a wife. He was only in his early twenties, but he had dreamed of getting married ever since he was a young teenager. He knew a wife was a gift from God, and he had watched how much in love his parents had been growing up. He could hardly wait to have such a special bond with one person.

If only his parents were still alive. Even if Elijah did have children one day, they would only have one set of grandparents. How Elijah's parents would have loved to have grandchildren. At least he had Esther and Irvin Holt. They were almost like parents to him. But even with the Holts right next door, he still felt lonely sometimes.

"At least I have You, Lord," Elijah said quietly.

He opened his Bible to see his familiar bookmark. His fingers brushed the waxy paper of the lollipop wrapper he had saved from his childhood. He had eaten the little orange sucker right away, since it was such a rare treat. But even after all these years, he could still not part with the simple wrapper.

Maybe it was silly. Over a decade had passed since that blonde *Englisher* girl had given it to him. How long had it been? Twelve years? Fifteen years? Her name was Charlie, short for Charlotte. He knew he'd never forget it because it was such an odd nickname for a girl. He remembered her laughing eyes. And the strange, exciting feeling she had given him.

Over the years, Elijah had been interested in a few girls. But he'd never pursued any of them because he didn't feel God calling him to. He never felt the kind of connection with them that he'd experienced with that girl in the barn when he was ten years old. He longed to feel that way about a woman. Maybe it had just been feelings one only had during childhood, but whatever it was, it had felt so genuine.

All this time, he'd kept the wrapper as a reminder to pray for that girl

For over fifteen years, he'd asked God to bring Charlie back into his life.

As he turned the wrapper over in his calloused hands, he prayed, "Lord, please keep her safe, help her love you more every day, and help me also love you more than anything. And if you do bring her back to me, please help me not mess it up."

He set down his Bible and walked to the Holts' house for supper.

The aroma of beef stew warmed his insides as he stepped into the familiar kitchen. Esther was slicing her homemade bread at the table.

"Hello, Elijah."

"Hi, Esther. I was wondering, do you remember that young girl named Charlie and her mother who came here about fifteen years ago? She was blonde, and she and her mother were *Englishers*. Who were they?"

"I don't know what you're talking about." Esther cut into the bread with more force than necessary.

"It's hard to forget. Her mom was so upset when they left. In fact, she said you refused to speak to them and made them leave. What was that all about?" He knew he was prying, but the words had just tumbled out. He couldn't stop them. "And I remember her name was Charlie because it's such an odd name for a girl."

"It was no one, Elijah. It does not concern you," she said stiffly.

"What happened? Something must have happened for you to not want to talk to her. Will they come back?" he pressed, knowing he should stop talking, but he couldn't. "It's not like you at all to turn someone away at the door."

"It's a long story, one I don't care to revisit. I do not suspect they will ever come back. Now, do not ask me again," she said in such a firm voice that he jumped in surprise. Esther had always been a mild and sweet woman. What had made her so angry? Elijah had never seen her act like that before.

Elijah knew he was crossing the line by a mile, but he just had to know who the girl was. "Esther, please, I just want to know—"

Esther lifted her head slowly, looking him right in the eye, and set her knife down on the table with a thud.

"Elijah," she said in a pained, low voice. Her eyes narrowed, giving her an expression that was so unlike her usual smiling face. "The woman was my sister. I can't talk about what happened. I just can't. It's more complicated and terrible than you'll ever know. Don't ask me about her again."

***

The following night, Dad got a phone call from the hospital while they were having dinner at home. Since Dad was sitting close enough to her Charlie overheard the voice on the phone.

"Come to the hospital now. I'm afraid this could possibly be Joanna's last night," the woman on the phone told them.

"What's going on?" Zoe, Charlie's eight-year-old sister asked, looking between Charlie and their father. "Dad? Charlie?"

Dad just hung his head.

Charlie's eyes stung with tears as she patted her younger sister's hand. "We have to leave right now, Zoe. We have to go see Mom."

As Dad sped them to the hospital, Charlie said, "Dad, if you're going to drive like this, you really should wear your seat belt. I mean, you always should, but especially right now."

"You know I hate seat belts. There shouldn't even be a law that we have to wear them. It should be our own choice. And I hate how constricting they

146

are. Besides, that's the last thing on my mind right now. Let's not have this argument again tonight."

Charlie sighed. How many times had they argued about seat belts over the years? Even Mom had tried to get Dad to wear one, but he wouldn't budge.

They arrived at the hospital and rushed to Mom's room.

It all felt unreal as they entered the white room containing her frail mother. Charlie halted at the door.

She couldn't do this.

She felt her throat constrict, and for a moment her stomach felt sick. "No, Dad, I can't," she whispered, her hand on her stomach. "I can't say goodbye."

"Charlie, this is your last chance. If you don't, you'll regret it forever. I know you can do it. You are made of the same stuff as your mother," he said and pulled her close, stroking her hair.

Compliments were rare from her father, but she was too heartbroken to truly appreciate it.

He let out a sob, and Charlie's heart wrenched. She hated it when her dad cried, which Charlie had only seen once or twice in her life. Zoe came over and wrapped her arms around them, then they walked over to the bed together.

They held her hand and whispered comforting words. They cried and laughed a little at fond memories. Her father said his goodbyes, Zoe said her goodbyes, and then it was Charlie's turn.

She did not bother trying to stop the flow of her tears. Sorrow crushed her spirit, and no matter how hard she tried she could not see how any silver lining could come from this. Was God punishing her for something? Why was He taking her beautiful, wonderful mother?

"Charlie, I love you," her mother whispered and clutched her hand with little strength.

"I love you too, Mom," Charlie choked out.

"Please promise me, Charlie. Chase your dreams and become a teacher."

"Okay, Mom. I will."

"I just want you to be happy."

"Mom, I will be. I promise."

"Take care of them."

"I will, Mom." She barely got the words out before another round of tears came.

"Thank you. I'll be watching."

Charlie nodded, unable to speak, biting her lip to keep from crying out.

"One more thing. There's something I need to tell you. Please tell your Aunt Esther that I forgive her. Promise me you will. And tell her I'm sorry. I am so sorry." Mom sobbed, and Charlie saw the same pain in her eyes she'd seen all those years ago after they left the Amish farm.

"Why, Mom? Sorry for what?"

"I lied to you yesterday, Charlie, when I said I wasn't angry with her. I didn't want you to think I was a bitter person. Honestly, I have been angry at her for years for shunning me. It was so hard to talk about. I'm so sorry I didn't tell you the whole story."

"It's okay, Mom. I love you."

"I love you too. Tell Esther I love her and that I'm sorry. I forgive her

I hope she forgives me too…" Regret shone in Mom's eyes, then her eyes fluttered closed and the monitor next to her started beeping loudly.

"Forgive you for what? Why does she need to forgive you?" Charlie asked, panic rising in her voice as her eyes darted to the monitor. "What's wrong? What's happening?"

"Her heart rate is dropping," the nurse said and called the doctor into the room.

Charlie's heart wrenched at the sight of Zoe weeping, begging Mom not to die. Dad reached for Mom.

"Mom!" Zoe screamed.

"I'm sorry," the nurse said to Dad. "This could be it."

The doctor assessed her and slowly shook his head, frowning. "I'm so sorry. We tried everything we could. There's nothing more we can do. We will give you some privacy. Please call us if you need anything. We are right down the hall."

Charlie stood on shaky legs, feeling like they would give out at any moment. The doctor continued talking, but his words sounded like muffled gibberish in her ears. He turned and walked out of the room.

Charlie squeezed Mom's hand. "Mom? Mom? Please, tell me what you want Aunt Esther to forgive you for." It seemed so important to Mom, and Charlie wasn't sure if Dad would talk about it, so this could be her last chance to find out. If Mom's dying wish was to ask Aunt Esther's forgiveness for something, Charlie wanted to honor it.

Mom barely opened her eyes and mumbled something incoherent.

"Joanna, we are all here." Dad took Mom's other hand, and Zoe stood by Mom's bed.

Then Mom managed to whisper, "I…love…you…all." Her eyes opened for one fleeting moment, and she looked at each of them. She gave a small smile. "I'm going with Jesus." Her eyes closed.

The machine beside them made one long beeping sound.

She was gone.

Zoe cried out. They held each other as they wept.

Charlie's heart felt literally broken. She sucked in some air, feeling her chest ache, as if there was no air left to breathe.

When they finally left the hospital, she was in a haze as her feet moved on auto pilot. After they got to the apartment, hours passed before they finished drying their tears.

What would Mom say to make her feel better? That this was God's will? Charlie knew that was exactly what she'd say.

Why did God *want* this to happen?

Why didn't He take me instead? Mom was so…good, she thought glumly.

Her whole life she had been taught about the perfect love of Jesus and His wonderful plan for her life. Why was this part of His plan? This was not a wonderful plan.

She fell on her bed, put her head down on her pillow and sighed. "God…please just help me get through this. I don't know what to think right now. Please help me stop doubting you and just trust You."

Someone knocked on the apartment door. When neither her father nor Zoe got up to see who it was, Charlie dragged herself off her bed and went to the door, opening it.

"Alex!" she cried in surprise.

Her ex-fiancé stood in the doorway in his crisp police uniform. Dad and Zoe quickly came over to see what was going on.

"I need to talk to you, Charlie," he told her with determination. He glanced at Charlie's dad and sister. "Alone."

"Not going to happen, Alex," Dad said, stomping towards Alex. "In fact, you broke my daughter's heart. You cheated on her. If she doesn't want to talk to you, she doesn't have to."

"This is terrible timing, Alex. My mother just passed away," Charlie told him, tears constricting her voice. "You should go."

"I'm really sorry. But I've got to tell you something important, Charlie," Alex insisted, taking hold of Charlie's arm a little too roughly. "Come talk to me in the hallway for one minute."

"No." Charlie shoved him away.

"Charlie!" Alex yelled and pulled on her arm again, harder this time. "Come on. I wouldn't be here if it wasn't really important."

"Enough. Get out of here right now, Alex. And don't come back, you hear?" Dad's tall, daunting form seemed to take up the entire doorway. He loomed over Alex threateningly.

The police officer backed away with his hands up and stormed down the stairs.

Charlie let out a sigh of relief. He was gone. For now.

*

If you enjoyed this sample, check out Amish Alias by Ashley Emma here on Amazon:

https://www.amazon.com/Amish-Alias-Romantic-Suspense-Detectives-ebook/dp/B07ZCJBWJL

Printed in Great Britain
by Amazon